RISING DAWN

A DARK DYSTOPIAN OMEGAVERSE

DAWN OF THE ALPHA
BOOK 1

SINISTRE ANGE

1

DEATH IN THE STREET

Jordan

Blood exploded in his mouth, sharp and coppery. His jaw throbbed from the force of the blow. He strained, but the grip holding his arms behind his back was too strong.

Cowards.

They were no true Alphas. If they were, they would have had no need of the other's help. A challenge of single combat would not be forthcoming. They were not here for dominance, they were here as assassins, sent by his father. Another coward, another Alpha in name only, for all that he ruled over the entire territory.

Jordan growled, his muscles clenching, surging. Pain tore at his ligaments, stretching his shoulders as the males holding him tightened their grips. It would not be a quick death and he knew it. His would be a death with a message in it.

See how merciless I am to my own son, my heir. Think of what I would do to you *if you dare cross me.*

Not that his father had the guts to actually get his own hands bloody. Likely he was safely ensconced in his harem of Omegas, fucking and rutting to his heart's content, and waiting to hear from the captain of his guard that it was done. The same captain who now grinned wildly at Jordan, fire in his dark eyes as he raised his fist again.

Jordan spit blood in his smug face. He was pinioned in place, unable to move a single limb, but he would not go down without some sort of resistance.

Snarling, the male swiped his arm across his cheek, smearing the red across his skin.

"Whelp."

He backhanded Jordan, hard enough to snap his head back. In a true challenge, Jordan would have gutted him easily and they both knew it. That was why Morpheus hated him. One too many times shown up in the training arena and this was how he acted.

"Beta," Jordan snapped back, feeling the blood dripping down over his lip, across his chin and then to the dusty street. Morpheus' eyes flared with anger. The fingers gripping Jordan tightened even more, pain streaking through him as Morpheus' men pulled, his joints creaking in protest. "Hell, you might as well be an Omega in my father's harem, you're practically gagging on his cock already."

The flurry of blows to his stomach drove the breath from him, his kidneys screaming in pain. Another fist to his face, plowing through, rattling his teeth and breaking his cheekbone. The crunch was sickening.

"Beg, whelp, and maybe we'll let you live." Morpheus' offer was as unappealing as it was empty. Only a fool would have believed him, but many became fools in the face of inevitable death, grasping at even the faintest of false hopes.

Jordan laughed, blood bubbling up in his mouth, spewing out from between his lips. It was the funniest damned thing he'd ever heard. No matter that Morpheus had been the one to initially train Jordan himself, that he'd been around since Jordan truly was a whelp, he'd never understood him and he never would.

Another blow that snapped his head around. He laughed harder. The sound was unnervingly raw, and more than one of the males holding him shivered. They had all faced him, singularly, in the training arena and knew they would never have beaten him there.

Even now they feared he would somehow rally and overpower them. But he knew he couldn't.

Death was coming, ruining all his plans, all his careful strategies for the future, and his hopes for vengeance, but still he laughed. There was nothing else to do.

FROM DOWN THE STREET HE WATCHED THE SON OF JEFFOS BEING BEATEN to death. While he had no love for the Warlord's family, he had to admit he was impressed. The whelp was young. Eighteen at best. Yet he laughed, spewing blood and spit on his murderers.

Five full trained Alphas on the Warguard against one youth?

Even if they hadn't sprung a trap on him, the young Alpha would have been hard pressed to defend himself. Now he was pinioned, one guard holding one limb apiece, keeping him spread eagle. They pulled at him, as though they were going to tear him apart, limb from limb, while their captain pummeled his body and face.

The sound of his laughter echoed down the otherwise empty street.

When the guard had appeared, the betas who usually occupied these sidewalks had scattered.

He had remained, hidden in the shadows where he'd been watching the guard already, wondering what they'd been doing. When they'd sprung the trap, he'd been surprised. The young Alpha was known to everyone in the Warlord's Territory, by sight.

He hadn't expected Jeffos' son to be their prey.

Nor that Jeffos would have sent them.

Curiouser and curiouser.

The young male likely wouldn't last much longer. Even now his laughter was growing weaker, fading with every hard blow to his body and face.

He had a decision to make.

JORDAN

Pain and blood.

Somehow it seemed fitting that this was his end. The same one he'd meant for his father. Perhaps the old bastard had been right, and to plot against him *was* a sin. Perhaps this was Jordan's just punishment for wanting to overthrow his own sire.

The world was becoming cloudy. His ears were ringing and he could no longer tell what Morpheus or the others were saying. The laughter that had run out so clearly now bubbled in his throat with wet gasps as he swallowed some of the blood that was pouring out of his mouth. Agony exploded all over his body, bursting with sharp edges that cut into him and began to fade only for a new spot to erupt when Morpheus landed another blow.

Then it ceased.

He drew in a deep breath. Nearly screamed at the pain from the attempt.

His lungs were no longer working properly.

The ringing in his receded slightly.

"Lift up his head." Morpheus' cruel voice, laced with sick satisfaction. "I want to be the last thing he sees."

Ha. Another laugh burbled wetly in Jordan's throat. Joke was on Morpheus. Jordan could barely see anything.

But fingers yanked on his hair, pulling his head upright.

Blurry vision slowly came into focus in his right eye, though the left was too damaged to see more than light and shadows. Morpheus smirked at him.

"Last chance to beg, whelp."

Jordan blinked. His tongue was too swollen to answer even if he wanted to.

Which he didn't. He would never give Morpheus the satisfaction. Nor was he looking at Morpheus because Morpheus wanted him to. He was doing it to show Morpheus how a true Alpha behaved, not a sniveling weakling who could only best another Alpha with help.

As if realizing his demand wasn't working the way Morpheus had thought it would, the captain seemed unnerved by Jordan's stare.

Despite his broken nose, Jordan could almost smell the craven Alpha's fear.

Because his head was lifted, he also saw something flying through the air. He couldn't flinch, held as tightly as he was, and it hit the guard beside him with a wet *thunk.* The hand holding his head up fell away, the arm bracing his left arm dropping along with the guard.

One hand was now free.

A shadow rushed at Morpheus, who snarled with anger and fear at the sudden attack. The guards holding Jordan shouted, loosening their grip, rushing at whoever was coming to Jordan's defense.

Half-blind, bruised all over, and barely able to breathe, Jordan still managed to catch one of them by the leg as he fell, causing them to trip on his way down. He owed that much to his savior.

The ground rushed up and he cried out in pain when he landed on the hard stone of the street. The smell of his own blood filled his nose from where it pooled on the ground next to him. It was spattered across the stones, speckling it.

The roars and growls of Alphas fighting – a true battle, unlike the beating Morpheus had implemented on him – filled the air.

The guard whose leg Jordan had caught kicked him in the face and he released the male's ankle, no longer able to hold on. He'd done what he could. Now he would die on the ground from his wounds, rather than from Morpheus' hand, denying the captain his revenge, and there was some satisfaction in that.

At least, he hoped he died before Morpheus and the guards dealt with the interloper.

Though Jordan knew he could best them, or could have if they hadn't ambushed him, he did not hold out much hope for anyone else. His savior would pay for their kindness with their life, but there was nothing he could do about that.

So it was with great surprise that when the snarls and growls died out, the sound of footsteps fleeing down the street rang out, and then a gentle hand touched his head.

He opened his right eye. The left was now swollen shut, crusted and throbbing with pain.

Bright green eyes met his. The huge male peering at him was clearly an Alpha. It showed in every line of his body, the square precision of his jaw, the aura of confident authority that hung about him.

"I can save you." The green eyes bore into Jordan, drilling down into his own gaze, like the male was looking inside his soul. There was strength in his gaze, but no kindness. He was no Good Samaritan. Behind him, the bodies of Morpheus' guards lay. The captain had fled from this male, utterly defeated. "Swear fealty to me and I will."

"Who... are... you?" Jordan forced the words out.

For a long moment the male paused, studying him, and then he nodded. A short, sharp movement.

"You may call me Malachi."

2

BRAVERY & STUPIDITY

Tatiana

"Where is Malachi?"

Jerking her head up, Tatiana dropped it down just as quickly as Cora and Trace came striding into the room. The two Alphas were always kind to her, but sometimes the way they looked at her... she was an unclaimed Omega after all. Because Malachi refused to claim her.

"Out," Grigori said dismissively, not even looking up from where he was sitting reading, much less getting to his feet in the presence of the Alphas. Tatiana shot him a worried glance as she stood to acknowledge the visiting Alphas, but it was already too late.

While Trace could be described as easy going, for an Alpha, Cora was not and she was across the room in a moment, her hand wrapped around Grigori's throat as she easily lifted the beta off his feet.

"Is that how you speak to an Alpha, beta?" The beads at the end of her braids clicked ominously, swinging behind her as she swayed slightly, her dark eyes filled with contempt.

"Please, Alpha, he forgot himself," Tatiana said, taking a step away from the window seat where she'd been sitting, watching and waiting for Malachi to return.

"That is nothing new, Tatiana," Cora said, tilting her head up at Grigori, whose reddening face was starting to turn purplish. He kicked his legs out uselessly, hands clawing at his throat. Across the room, Trace crossed heavy arms over his chest, watching the scene with impassive eyes. "It's a wonder Malachi hasn't killed him yet. There is no place here for a rebellious beta."

"Please," Tatiana begged, tears starting to form in her eyes. She deliberately added a low purr to her voice, the kind of sound only an Omega could make, meant to soothe a riled Alpha. It was manipulative... but she couldn't let Cora kill Grigori if she could help it, no matter how disrespectful and rebellious he'd become. She owed him too much.

Pursing her lips, Cora let him drop in a gasping heap on the floor, a huddle of unhappy limbs, choking for air.

"Next time, think before you speak, beta. One of these days your friendship with Tatiana is not going to be enough to save you."

Tears sparked in Tatiana's eyes, because she knew what Cora said was true. Grigori resented that he wasn't an Alpha and he was becoming bolder in his insolence when dealing with them. Unfortunately, as a beta, he didn't have the muscle or the instincts to challenge them.

She didn't know where he got the bravery either.

Then again, she was an Omega, but she couldn't imagine challenging any of them even if she was a beta. Cora was a head taller than Grigori, her muscles more pronounced. The gleaming gold band against her dark skin on her bicep emphasized that fact even more. Trace was even more intimidating. Where Grigori was lanky, Trace was built like a tank, his bulging muscles putting even Malachi's to shame – though the two were evenly matched when they sparred thanks to Malachi's almost unnatural speed.

Trace also had the darkest skin Tatiana had ever seen, making Grigori look sickly pale beside him, his blond hair limp and washed out, his complexion pallid. Everything about Grigori screamed 'beta' except his attitude.

Sweeping her braids back over her shoulder with a series of tiny clicks, Cora turned her attention to Tatiana.

"And you are doing him no favors by interceding for him, little Omega," she admonished, though her tone was gentle. Tatiana ducked her head. She knew Cora was right. One day one of the Alphas visiting Malachi wouldn't care what Grigori meant to Tatiana and they would demand real retribution for Grigori's lack of respect no matter how Tatiana begged. It was only due to Cora and Trace's long friendship with Malachi, and his devotion to Tatiana, that they allowed her to plead Grigori's case... which made him ever-bolder.

"Malachi went out to scout the streets," Tatiana said, changing the subject rather than answering Cora's scolding. The Alpha shook her head at Tatiana's tactics but allowed the diversion. Tatiana knew that she was shamelessly indulged by all the Alphas, and she tried not to take advantage of it... too much.

"Do you know when he'll be back?" Cora watched as Tatiana's gaze slid back to Grigori, who was finally sitting up, massaging his throat. He was now pink instead of purple, and smart enough to keep his gaze downcast rather than glaring at Cora. Trace was watching him closely, as if waiting for just such an opportunity. Cora rolled her eyes. "Oh, go check on him then."

"He said he would be back in time to eat," Tatiana said, glancing at the clock as she hurried over to Grigori. Though, with Malachi, that could mean anytime between eleven and one, which was why she'd been sitting and watching for his return, despite Grigori's attempts to engage her. He didn't approve of her devotion to Malachi. He didn't understand it.

When Tatiana knelt next to him, he didn't look at her either.

"Let me see," she said softly, gently trying to tug his fingers away from her throat.

"What do you care?" His tone was harsh, bitter, but quiet. Cowed. At least for now.

Across the room, Cora shifted on her feet, the movement enough to draw both Grigori and Tatiana's attention. As Malachi's Omega, unclaimed though she was, Tatiana was considered important by

Cora and Trace. To touch her without permission, to disrespect her, would mean a bloody death – as one visiting Alpha had learned to his detriment. His replacement had been much more respectful to her.

When they were alone, Tatiana did not ask Grigori to stand on ceremony, but he should know better with Malachi's two closest allies in the room. It was his bitterness that was making him stupid.

"Of course, I care, otherwise I would not have asked her to stop," Tatiana murmured, inspecting his throat. The damage was not bad. Cora had been careful not to crush his windpipe, though she easily could have. Grigori was too busy lamenting everything he did not have, he did not take the time to consider what he did.

Their lives had been so much worse before Malachi had found her. Grigori had saved her first, but Malachi had saved both of them. They owed him everything. Something that also made Grigori bitter. He was so busy lamenting everything that he was not, he couldn't appreciate everything they had.

"Can you tilt your head back?" When he did, gingerly, she nodded, relieved. "You will be fine. We should put some ice on your throat to help reduce the swelling though."

"Malachi is back." Trace's deep, rumbling announcement made Tatiana jump to her feet in happiness, already whirling around toward the window where Trace was now standing, peering out. "He's carrying someone. They look injured."

Immediately, Tatiana rushed out of the room. If Malachi was carrying someone injured back to their compound, it was because they needed her help.

Grigori

Once, he had not been so easily cast aside and forgotten.

Remembering the days when it had been him and Tatiana, without any of these Alphas ruining things, always brought a surge of bitterness welling in his chest, leaving a sour taste in his mouth. His throat ached, and he gently pressed the ice pack to it. The ice Tatiana had forgotten about as soon as her precious Malachi had returned.

Sliding into the main room of the house, he kept to the side, watching as Tatiana worked on the injured male Malachi had brought back. Her skills as a healer were second-to-none, and utterly wasted as the favored Omega of an Alpha in the territories. Especially *this* territory. She didn't seem to understand that Malachi was using her and her skills as he built up his army, marshaling his forces to challenge Jeffos.

The scent of a new Alpha filled the air, along with the coppery smell of blood and the dank musk of sweat. Grigori wrinkled his nose. It looked like the male had been beaten to death. It was a wonder he was still alive.

On the other side of the room, Cora watched impassively as Trace helped Malachi hold down the injured Alpha so that Tatiana could stitch him up. They didn't have any painkillers on hand. Well, none that Tatiana and the others knew about. Grigori had his own stash, which he was not willing to share. He'd already taken some for his throat. With as violent as the Alphas were, it was prudent to have his own supply.

Tatiana impatiently swept back her long fall of brown hair. It was always down, because that was how Malachi preferred it, even though it was constantly getting in her way. Especially now.

Grigori sighed inwardly. Time for him to step up and help her again, since Malachi's preferences were so impractical.

Pulling an elastic band from his pocket, he put down the ice and moved behind her, his hands scooping up the thick mass of her hair. Malachi's head came up, green eyes flashing under black eyebrows, his jaw tightening, but he didn't say anything. Anyone else touching Tatiana without his permission would be dealt with summarily, but Tatiana had made it clear that Grigori was her friend, and she didn't want Malachi to punish him for that.

Holding back his smirk, Grigori kept his face impassive as he arranged her hair, enjoying the feel of the silky strands sliding through his fingers. He lingered as much as he dared, knowing that

Malachi's possessive instincts would only allow so much latitude. At least Tatiana wasn't claimed. Then Malachi wouldn't have tolerated Grigori touching her at all, even though he was a beta.

Her unclaimed status also gave him hope. Eventually he would be able to convince her to escape the territories with him and go to the zones. Everyone there took suppressors and lived like betas. They could be free of the Alphas and the territories and her base nature... he just had to convince her.

Finishing off the ponytail, Grigori stepped away.

"He's been brutalized," Tatiana said, worry threaded through her tone. "I don't know if I'll be able to save him."

"Do your best. I want him alive." It was an order, though gently given. Malachi never issued orders to Tatiana about her patients, certainly not one as inane as telling her to save someone who might not be able to be saved.

Curious, Grigori peered around her, trying to see the male's face. He gasped when he saw the shock of pale blond hair on the male's head. The Warlord's heir?! That was who Malachi wanted to save?

Stepping back, Grigori's mind was already churning with the possibilities... and he happened to catch Cora's eye. He immediately dropped his head, the skin on his throat tingling as if with remembrance or warning, but he'd seen the expression on her face. She wasn't happy with Malachi's attempts to save Jeffos' son.

Grigori's thoughts raced. He could use this.

3

GRIGORI'S VOW

Tatiana

The young Alpha was horrifically injured.

Tatiana's hands shook as she set thread to needle and stitched up the worst of the wounds she'd cleaned. She knew who he was, of course. The hair gave it away. Hopefully, he was nothing like his father. She could not imagine Malachi bringing him back here if he was. There was nothing to fear. Malachi would protect her, as would Cora and Trace, but... her hands still shook.

When Grigori pulled her hair back out of her way, she shot him a grateful glance. Malachi and Trace were both busy holding down the young male, who was very strong despite being so injured. He did not like the needle moving through his skin, and she could not blame him. Unfortunately, they had nothing to numb the pain. She did not feel any better when he went limp.

Malachi wanted to save him. Using the back of her hand to wipe the sweat away from her brow, she stitched as fast as she could, then put poultices over the worst of the wounds and his eye, which was swollen beyond belief. The young male was pale and drawn by the time she finished, even paler than normal, but he looked more peaceful. Almost as if he was sleeping.

"Will he live?" Malachi asked, his voice a deep rumble as he came up alongside her, his hand coming to rest possessively on the back of her neck. Fingers caressed, then massaged, rubbing away the worst of her tension. Sighing, Tatiana leaned against him, letting his strength hold her up.

"Maybe." She didn't feel confident, but he had a chance. "He is young. Strong. You got him here before he had lost too much blood."

"Perhaps we should talk about *why* you brought him here, Malachi." Cora's voice whipped out, full of barely suppressed disapproval. Though she and Malachi were longtime allies, they butted heads regularly. Cora had recently secured leadership of her own territory, with Malachi's help, which was why she was here to help Malachi.

Why Malachi specifically wanted the Warlord's territory, no one knew. He'd been willing to help fight Cora's battles, standing aside and protecting her back when she challenged the old Alpha of the Riversong Territory, rather than challenging the Alpha himself.

"Morpheus and some warguards were beating him to death in the street." Malachi's tone was conversational as if he was merely commenting on the weather. His fingers still massaged Tatiana's neck, but everyone else in the room stilled. She exchanged a wide-eyed look with Grigori, whose mouth had dropped open in shock.

"His own son?" Every time Tatiana thought she was out of ways to be horrified by Jeffos' cruelty, but he would prove her wrong yet again.

"He truly cares for no one but himself," Trace said, shaking his head. Unlike the rest of them, Trace did not appear shocked, though there was disgust in his voice and expression.

"Why?" Cora mused. They all looked down at the young male, unconscious on the table. There was no doubt he should have died today. Without Malachi's interference, he would have. "He rarely does anything without reason anymore, even if the reason is to entertain himself. Why would he exert himself to kill off his heir?"

"Perhaps his heir was looking to depose him sooner rather than later?" Trace raised his eyebrow, heavy arms crossed over his chest as his eyes scanned over the unconscious male, assessing him. He ran one hand over his closely cropped black curls, lips pressing together thoughtfully as his eyes unfocused.

Though he was an Alpha, Trace had always seemed content to be Cora's right-hand man. He was the long-term strategist, while she was the tactician. They balanced each other in a way Tatiana envied. Cora was quick to action, while Trace took his time, holding her back from acting too impulsively, while she kept him from standing by on the sidelines, always watching and never acting.

Tatiana wanted to be that for Malachi, but he did not seem to need balance. He was neither as quick to act as Cora nor as slow to make a decision as Trace. While he had a long-term strategy, he had never shared it with her, but she knew enough to know his tactics changed daily, depending on what was thrown at him. He was never slow to make use of an unexpected opportunity, reveling in chaotic situations rather than thrown by them.

The only thing he ever seemed to need her for was sex and healing. At least he needed her for something.

"If that's true, Jeffos likely intended to make an example of him," she said, looking down at the young male. "He will look for him."

"Yes, he will." Malachi's fingers tightened briefly on her neck. Tatiana tipped her head back to look up at him. He was looking down at Jeffos' hair, grinning wolfishly. The times Malachi smiled were few and far between and usually at her. This was nothing like his usual smiles. Tatiana shivered.

<u>GRIGORI</u>

If the Warlord wanted his son dead...

Grigori rejected the idea of leading the Warguard here. It would put Tatiana in far too much danger. She never left the compound Malachi had made his headquarters. Though there was always a chance they could escape in the confusion, it was still far too risky. He had already saved her from being taken to join Jeffos' harem. He would not be the reason she ended up there.

If she disappeared into Jeffos' estate, there would be no way to find her. At least here, they could spend time together. He rubbed his throat, which still ached. He wouldn't mind sending Jeffos' men after Cora. Perhaps he could tell them the heir was in Riversong Territory... but he would also risk his own skin to approach them.

His next move would require some time, but he was accustomed to being patient to get what he wanted.

Noise outside made him step back against the wall. It was impossible to fade into the shadows, but he recognized the sound of Zadia's voice. Young, dumb, and desperate to prove herself to Malachi, the young Alpha female hated Grigori with a passion. Everyone liked to forget if it wasn't for him, they wouldn't have Tatiana. Ungrateful assholes.

Zadia came striding in with several of her betas. Her braided dark brown hair was coiled into a bun on the back of her head. Like the betas, she was garbed in black and green, a green armband with a stylized wolf's head wrapped around her left arm. She would be beautiful if she wasn't such an Alpha bitch.

Thankfully, she didn't see Grigori on the side of the room, her focus entirely on Malachi. Grigori was sure she wanted to fuck him and be the Alpha queen to his king, the way Cora and Trace were, but she was smart enough never to be unkind to Tatiana. Even if they paired up, Malachi would never willingly give up Tatiana, and they all knew it... but as long as Tatiana was unclaimed, Zadia and Grigori could have hope.

They had that in common, which was why Grigori had once hoped she'd be an ally. Too bad she was a cunt.

"Malachi." Her voice was reverent as she bowed her head in acknowledgment of his superiority. Standing there like a king, his hand still on Tatiana's neck while she leaned on him, Malachi nodded at Zadia. "You summoned me?"

Hm, interesting. Malachi must have done so as soon as he arrived, probably sending the guards at the gates to fetch her.

"I need you and your betas to go into the streets. Watch for the warguard. I want to know if anyone is saying anything about Jeffos' son."

Zadia lifted her head in surprise and stared straight at Malachi, ignoring Tatiana. Cunt.

"Jeffos' son? Jordan?"

That's right, that was the whelp's name—interesting that Zadia knew it. Grigori studied her more carefully.

"Yes. He's going to be our guest for a while." Malachi gestured behind him.

It was evident Zadia had been so preoccupied with Malachi, she hadn't noticed the big male lying on the table. Grigori sneered from his spot by the wall. Though he knew Zadia was not unobservant, as long as Malachi was in the room, she was blind to all else, not a trait that served her well.

Her mouth popped open in a surprised 'o' while the betas behind her looked equally startled and perhaps a little anxious. They were smarter than she was. Not surprising. The Alphas always underestimated him and the other betas. Superior bastards.

"Whatever they're saying, I want to know." Malachi's voice had turned dismissive.

Zadia snapped back to attention, nodding. Her gaze moved to Tatiana for a moment, expression impassive, before she spun away. Gesturing to her betas, she led them out of the room. Grigori lifted his lip in a sneer as she went.

Stepping forward, his movement drew Malachi's gaze. The sharp green eyes bore into him, and Malachi lifted one eyebrow.

"I will go as well," Grigori said. "I have some information sources who will only speak with me." It was true. He may not share everything he learned with Malachi but would likely share some. It was always good to remind Malachi he could be useful to keep around, besides keeping Tatiana happy. It irked Grigori that Malachi and the others valued him only for his friendship with Tatiana.

Malachi nodded, his expression blank. Grigori knew the Alpha was doubting Grigori could learn anything. Gritting his teeth, Grigori smiled back at Tatiana, who was beaming at him. If nothing else, that would bother Malachi. Tatiana's approval and belief in him washed over him like a balm, though it did not entirely soothe the sting of the Alpha's contempt.

Turning to leave, Grigori ignored the look Trace and Cora exchanged.

One day he'd show them. One day he'd show them all.

4

THE THWARTED WARLORD

Jeffos

Sweet juices poured over his fingers as he moved them inside the Omega sitting on his lap. The redhead was his current favorite and possibly the bearer of his next heir. She whimpered and her muscles quivered around his thick digits as he loosened her hole, readying it for his cock.

"My lord, Morpheus has returned."

Raising his gaze from the reddened, swollen lips gripping his fingers, Jeffos continued to pump his fingers into the Omega as he acknowledged his guard's words. He smirked at the expression on the Alpha's face, the clear lust blazing in his eyes, for all that he was determinedly not looking at the little Omega. His own cock ached, but he liked to put on these little shows for his males to remind them of what they wanted.

Whoever controlled the Omegas controlled the Alphas, which was why Jeffos had made sure all the Omegas were rounded up and added to his harem. Although he preferred the females for himself, he had males, females, and several Omegas who were both and neither. Whatever his Alphas desired, he would provide them with—as long as they were worthy.

This particular guard had done nothing of note, so he was consigned to standing outside Jeffos' throne room, able to hear the moans of pleasure and smell the sweet slick pouring from the Omega's eager pussy. To touch one of Jeffos' harem without his permission was death, and those without the willpower to control themselves weren't worthy of being part of his guard.

All things considered, this guard was doing an admirable job of pretending the Omega's scent had no effect on him. Perhaps Jeffos would reward him by giving him the opportunity to prove himself and earn the services of an Omega to satisfy his cock.

"Send him in." Settling back into his throne, Jeffos cast his gaze over the Omega kneeling on his lap, her thighs spread wide, waiting for him to finish with his fingers so he could fuck her. Ankles crossed between his knees, her arms behind her back, so her pert breasts were thrust out in front of his face, she was an alluring sight.

Well-trained, too. She'd barely flinched when she learned their audience would be increasing. Then again, as her own need to be fucked and knotted rose, she would care less and less about their surroundings, her arousal encompassing and overshadowing all other concerns.

The moment Morpheus entered the throne room, Jeffos knew his captain had failed, and his son was not dead.

He growled, his fingers curving and hooking inside the Omega on his lap. She cried out in pain but did not move, and he rewarded her by letting his fingers straighten again, his thumb brushing over her clit.

Dark fury still pulsed as he stared at his battered Captain of the Warguard. Other than himself and his son, Morpheus was the deadliest Alpha in his territory, yet here he was, looking worse for the wear and without the guards he'd taken with him to take care of Jordan. Perhaps Jeffos should have taken care of the problem himself, but it suited him to be underestimated.

He knew the rumors in his territory about his laziness and self-indulgence. After all, he had been the one to cultivate them.

"What happened?" His voice came out in a growl rather than the lazy drawl he usually used when granting an audience. The guards at the door stiffened. They were far away, at the other end of the room, but Jeffos noticed. Jeffos noticed everything.

Like the blood smeared across Morpheus' cheek, the limp he was vainly trying to hide in order to appear strong, and the way he couldn't quite straighten up, as if he'd taken too many blows to his torso. Jeffos mentally catalogued every weakness in his head, the way he always did.

Everyone's strengths, everyone's weaknesses. The only one who had ever concerned him was his own son, whose betrayal had finally been uncovered. The whelp always had been far too attached to his mother. The next time Jeffos bred an heir, he would remove the mother from the situation immediately. He never made the same mistake twice.

First, he needed to take care of Jordan before he could concentrate on breeding and raising his replacement.

Even damaged, Morpheus' eyes slid over the Omega's back and buttocks, attracted by her mere scent. Yet other than that brief look and the bulge in the front of his pants swelling, he had no reaction.

"We were attacked." Morpheus' report was straight and to the point. Other than his strength as an Alpha, it was another reason Jeffos had chosen him to be captain. He didn't bullshit, and he didn't make excuses. He also didn't take defeat kindly. After realizing Jordan could best him on a level playing field, his pride had taken a hit, and he'd been more than willing to help remove the threat to his dominance.

Morpheus was only willing to bow to one master—Jeffos. Since that suited Jeffos, he kept Morpheus in his position.

"I beat Jordan to within an inch of his life and was about to land the killing blow when an unknown Alpha male attacked us."

An Alpha.

For the first time, Jeffos' fingers slowed, his movements decreasing as his need to focus increased. The Omega on his lap whimpered and wiggled a little but otherwise remained in place. Not that it would help her. His own anger about his plans being upended was sending him into a righteous fury, and he would take it out on her body once he was done getting Morpheus' report.

The only way another Alpha would have intervened with the Warguard was if they were in a league together. How far had Jordan got in his plans to overthrow Jeffos? How many allies did he have?

Reaching up, he cupped the Omega's breast, pinching her nipple hard enough to make her cry out. Her muscles spasmed around his fingers, another gush of slick coating them as the pain aroused her further. The sound of her pain made him feel a little better. It always did.

"Black hair, green eyes, at least my height. He's had training." Morpheus paused, then shook his head. "Something about him was vaguely familiar, but I didn't recognize him. I would guess in his thirties."

"He defeated you."

A snarl erupted from Morpheus' chest before he could suppress it. The male didn't like to hear the words, no matter the truth of them.

"He killed my men." The words were said flatly. "I deemed it better to retreat with information." From someone else, that might have sounded like an excuse. From Morpheus, it was likely nothing but pure fact... perhaps a touch of self-preservation. Morpheus and Jeffos were alike in that way, preferring to attack only when they were sure they could win. Which was why Morpheus had never challenged him.

"The last I saw, the unknown Alpha was carrying Jordan away. With the wounds he had, it is likely he will be dead soon, anyway."

Jeffos didn't deal in 'likely' and 'probably.' He wanted certainty, especially when it came to his upstart son. Jordan's slow and painful death was supposed to be an example of what happened to those who dared to go against him. Instead, if anyone found out Morpheus had been defeated and Jordan rescued...

"Find them." The words came out in a snarl. "Gather whatever males you need. Find Jordan and this unknown Alpha. I want their heads on spikes."

Morpheus nodded jerkily and turned away as Jeffos returned his attention to the Omega perched atop him.

Coldly, he reached up and curled his fingers around her throat, using her slender neck to pull her forward. Her pulse fluttered against his palm, eyes widening as she sucked in a short breath before he squeezed, cutting off her air and making her eyes bulge.

"Ride me well, and if you do a good enough job, perhaps I will let you live."

Perhaps. He had a good deal of pent-up aggression to work out. Relaxing his grip just enough to let her gasp for air, he shifted beneath her so she could impale herself on his cock, eyes glassy with fear the entire time. He relished the scent of her terror, leaning in to breathe it in as her cunt spasmed pleasurably around him.

TATIANA

"He's doing better." Tatiana bent her head to the young male's chest, listening to his heartbeat, which was no longer as thready as it had originally been. His breath had evened out, and he was sleeping. Recovering. He was strong. She sighed with relief. He was likely going to live.

Straightening, she smiled at Malachi, whose lips lifted slightly.

"Good girl." The warmth in his tone sent a flush right through her, igniting a simmering heat that was never far away when Malachi was around. "Thank you for saving him."

Tatiana beamed at him.

"You two go on." Cora waved her hand at them, settling into a chair on the side of the room. "Trace and I will keep watch over this one until he wakes up." Trace nodded, ambling over to lean against the wall on the other side of the Warlord's son, keeping the male between them. If he woke up violently, which wasn't too far out of the realm of possibility, they would already flank him.

Hopefully, if that occurred, they wouldn't undo any of her hard work. He should be too weak to fight effectively, so they should have no trouble subduing him.

A gentle hand slid up to cup the back of her neck, fingers caressing her throat. Tatiana's pulse sped up, her nipples puckering in anticipation as her arousal was roused with a mere touch.

"Yes. I think my sweet Tatiana deserves a reward." The compliment was accompanied by Malachi's purr, the rumble in his chest that called to her Omega instincts, making her weak and melty. She could already feel heat and wetness gathering between her thighs.

Turning to look up at him, she met his blazing green eyes and licked her lips. Malachi's smile widened, his thumb stroking along her jawline. He leaned down, brushing his lips against the top of her head. Even that small touch made her shiver in anticipation of the pleasure she knew he would give her.

5

REWARDING HIS OMEGA

Tatiana

Malachi's room was among the largest in their hideout, big enough for the huge bed Tatiana shared with him at night, a bookshelf, a desk, and a small sitting area. Technically, she had her own rooms, but she rarely used them. Even when Malachi was gone overnight, she preferred his. Her nesting instincts drove her to his space rather than hers.

On the bed was her latest nest, undisturbed, and her happy heart crooned at the sight of it still there, but she didn't have long to enjoy the sight. As soon as the door shut behind Malachi, he pulled her against him and claimed her lips in a deep, possessive kiss. Tatiana submitted to him, opening her lips for his tongue, her body bending against his as her hands rubbed his broad chest. She felt the rumble of his purr beneath her fingertips as much as she heard it, and her body quivered in response.

A gush of wet slick pulsed, coating the insides of her thighs. The scent of it filled the air around them, the sticky-sweet perfume of an Omega's lust and need, an aphrodisiac for the Alphas around her. But the only Alpha she wanted, the only male she'd ever wanted, was Malachi.

He dominated her completely, backing her step by step toward the bed, to her nest. It was the work of a moment to divest her of the simple dress she wore, leaving her bare for his touch, for his lust. Tatiana moaned as his hands moved over her body, cupping and squeezing her lush breasts, caressing her hips and bottom, igniting a needy heat deep between her legs. It was met by the need in her heart, the yearning for Malachi's bite, to be made his mate.

She knew better than to ask.

Going on his knees, he tipped her back onto the bed. Tatiana fell against her nest, a purr vibrating through her as the softness of the bed, pillows, and sheets cushioned her while Malachi spread her thighs. A hot, thick tongue laved between her lower lips, drinking her cream, making a feast of her desire.

The need that rose up, sharp and aching, pierced through her, leaving her breathless with hunger for him.

"Malachi..." Fingers threaded through his hair, she pulled him, trying to pull him up onto her, so she could have at his cock, her body aching and quivering to be filled and knotted, but he easily resisted. Licking and suckling, he tormented her with pleasure, giving her so much, although both of them knew it would not be enough.

His hands drifted up her body, arms beneath her thighs, spreading them wide with his shoulders, so he could cup and caress her breasts. Thumbs brushed against her nipples, teasing the tiny buds, adding more stimulation to the chaos already rioting through her.

He purred, the deep Alpha rumble sending a gush of fluid for him to lap up pouring from her. Tatiana writhed, a willing supplicant to the wave of lust, impatiently awaiting her fulfillment.

"Malachi, please!" Begging would do no good, it never had, yet she could not stop herself.

She burned.

Ached.

Throbbed.

Climax washed over her, resplendent rapture that made her cry out, twisting against his mouth while his tongue toyed with her clit, but it wasn't enough. She was so empty, empty, empty. Her inner muscles clenched and quivered around a cock that wasn't there, as if her spasm could make one appear to satisfy her body's craving.

Then he stood, looming over her, one hand fisting his shaft, pumping. A drop of liquid quivered on the end, the heavenly scent calling to her, and Tatiana reached for him.

"No, little one, lie back. Hands above your head." His voice was raspier, deeper than normal. Tatiana whimpered but obeyed, trusting her show of submission would tempt him far more than defiance.

With her hands up and her legs spread, she was bare to his gaze. Mounded breasts with their hard pink tips pointed to the ceiling, proffered up for his perusal. Tanned thighs spread wide, the sweet, dark pink flesh between them was swollen and glistening with her slick, ready to take him into her body and join them together as only Alpha and Omega could. She canted her hips upward, purring harder to tempt him with her exposed flesh.

"Good girl."

The accolade never failed to make her flush with pleasure, from the top of her head to the tips of her curling toes.

Climbing into her nest with her, dislodging some of the cushions, Malachi settled between her thighs. His lips met hers, bringing the taste of her own arousal to her tongue as his cock nudged against the entrance to her body. Tatiana moaned, licking his mouth, her muscles stretching to accommodate her Alpha's girth.

Rocking his hips, he pushed in deep, hard, just enough to hurt. The sting was delicious. She pushed her lower body up at him, wanting more. Hands slid under her shoulders, bracing her against him as he thrust, filling her completely with one sure stroke and making her cry out. The sound was muffled by his mouth as he drank in the noises she made as he rode her, the base of his cock already thickening and forming his knot.

It pulsed against the outside of her body, so wide and so unyielding. Despite being full to the brim with his flesh, she wanted more as she writhed beneath him in abject desire. Her whimpers met his growls, and with every noise he made, more slick poured from her, bathing his knot in her fluids, readying it for penetration.

Each hard thrust sent her senses soaring, and she finally could no longer hold back. Her hands moved, nails finding his shoulders and digging into the hard muscles. Tatiana screamed, her voice filling the room, along with Malachi's grunts and growls as he rutted her. His knot was pushing inside her, opening and stretching her so wide, she felt like she was going to split apart.

Her back bowed, hips pushing up to meet his thrusts, her inner muscles sucking and pulling until finally, his knot shoved inside of her, joining them completely. They rocked together as it expanded even more, pushing against the walls of her body as her muscles clenched around him.

Spasms of ecstasy wracked her, her muscles clamping around his shaft and pulsing, milking him. Malachi groaned, fully embedded inside her, his body jerking as he came with every convulsion of her cunt around his cock. The hard knot at its base throbbed inside her, her muscles pummeling it, pulling at it as she writhed in erotic bliss.

Teeth finding Malachi's skin, she sank them in, tasting blood as she bit his neck. She'd bitten him so many times, but without the return bite, their bond would never be complete. It did not matter. She needed to mark him as badly as she needed his cock inside her.

Shuddering, he growled, bowing his head before jerking it back, and she knew he was fighting his own instincts. Tears stung her eyes, but she blinked them back. Even though she did not agree with his reasons for leaving their bond incomplete, she understood them. Whether or not their lack of bond truly gave her any protection from those who might try to harm her to weaken him... well, she would tolerate what she had to in order to keep him.

One day, she promised herself... one day, they would be free of the Warlord's rule, and Malachi would fulfill his promise, and he would be hers.

SHE SLEPT IN HER RUINED NEST, THE SCENT OF HER SLICK AND HIS CUM hanging in the air around her. He knew she would rebuild it tomorrow and take great joy in doing so.

Watching her sleep was one of his few joys these days. So beautiful. So sweet. Completely sated, from being ridden and knotted. The only thing he couldn't give her—yet—was his bite.

His neck stung from where she'd sunk her teeth into his skin, and he relished the sensation. Regretted he could not return it. Not yet.

Not until Jeffos fell. When it would be safe for Tatiana to be his mate, claimed and acknowledged, rather than putting her in further danger. There would always be those who would try to use her against him, but being unmated gave her some small measure of protection.

Besides, he'd made a promise to Stasia, and Malachi always kept his promises.

6

MALACHI SENT US

Grigori

The streets of the Warlord's territory stank of fear and blood. It was no different from any other day, but today, there was an underlying thread of curiosity, of astonishment.

The Warlord's guard had tried to execute his son... and failed.

The Warguard was already out in force, doing its best to extinguish the tiny spark of excitement kindled at the news and making an example out of anyone who took courage from it. Grigori skirted one of the bodies in the street, too bloodied and pummeled to say anything about them other than they had been a Beta. He ground his teeth.

Fucking Alphas. What gave them the right? Betas were treated like trash, and it didn't matter if it was Jeffos or Malachi. Why couldn't Tatiana see that?

"Hey! You there! Stop!" Grigori glanced over his shoulder. To his relief, the Warguard was pointing at a female Beta, a little further down the street. She was frozen in terror.

Using the distraction to smoothly slip away into the shadows, Grigori hurried away, ignoring the pleas and screams that followed him as he left her to her fate. There was nothing he could do for her.

He didn't stand a chance against the Warguard, and he was not too proud to admit it.

He had to look out for himself first, which meant going to his next source of information, one of the Betas who worked in Jeffos' kitchens. While it was clear what Jeffos' reaction to the news of his son's rescue was, Grigori wanted to know what the old bastard was planning.

ZADIA

More of the Warguard were attacking a female Beta, shoving her back and forth between them and mocking her tears and screams. Fuckheads. Gritting her teeth, Zadia motioned to Marcus and Vin. They were both Betas, but they were highly trained Betas, and her favorite soldiers to work alongside. Alphas had an advantage in their sheer strength, speed, and ruthlessness, but they weren't invincible.

This would be the fourth congregation of assholes, Zadia and her small team would take care of today.

Marcus and Vin moved up on either side of her, flanking her so they could get clear shots. They'd be outnumbered, but that was nothing new.

Simultaneously, they threw their knives.

The steel hit with wet thunks and howls, three out of the seven guards flailing. Vin's and Marcus' targets went down after only a moment, while Zadia's turned, clutching the handle sticking out of his chest. Inwardly, she sighed. She didn't have the same accuracy as her Beta team. He was injured but not down for the count.

"This is great target practice!" Vin taunted, hefting another knife. "Try to move around a little more, make it harder on us."

This time, when he let the knife fly, the guard he was aiming for dodged it with a snarl, which was to be expected. It slammed into the shoulder of the male behind him, who howled with pain.

The five guards still on their feet, including the two injured, surged forward as a unit, anger easily overcoming the pain from the two with knives still sticking out of them. Behind them, the tearful Beta female hesitated instead of running. Brave but without training, likely to get herself killed.

"Split," Zadia murmured. They needed to lead these assholes away from the female, and hopefully, she would have the sense to abandon the scene and the two bodies lying in the street.

She ran down one street while Marcus and Vin took two others. This was the first time they had to split up, but they knew these streets like the back of their hands. There were predetermined meeting places where they could make another stand—the closest one was four streets away, and Zadia was taking the most circuitous route.

Glancing over her shoulder, she saw only one of the five chasing after her. Smirking, Zadia didn't bother to keep running. This street was already clear of passersby, though there were likely witnesses in the surrounding buildings. Let them see.

She turned, smirking when the Alpha following her pulled up fast and a little warily. Perhaps she shouldn't have been surprised it was the one her knife had hit, the hilt still sticking out of his chest.

Zadia stood with her feet well apart, hands held at the ready. She had another knife up her sleeve, and several more in various sheathes all over her person. Her own private collection of blades, perfect for slicing arrogant Alphas to ribbons.

"Alpha bitch." He snarled the words as if she cared what he thought.

"Shit gibbon," she threw back at him. Rather than waiting for him to attack, she bounded forward and saw his surprise when she caught him off guard. Idiots. The Warguard's biggest weakness was their overconfidence.

No one had fought back against them for so long, they'd forgotten *why* they traveled in groups.

The knife popped out of her forearm sheathe into her hand as she moved, then slashed at him. The guard stumbled back, his snarl twisting his features. Quick as a whip, she reached out and snatched the hilt from his chest, which had been her main goal. Now she was doubly armed, *and* his wound was no longer plugged.

A wet spot bloomed on his uniform where the knife had been. It would weaken him, but honestly, Zadia didn't intend to let him live long enough that the blood loss would make a difference to their fight.

"Bitch!"

"You already said that." Whirling, she kicked out, catching him on his hip and knocking him off balance. He spat at her and managed to catch her next kick, yanking her toward him with a light in his eyes. Even though they were both Alphas, he had at least fifty pounds of muscle on her, and she knew better than to get within grappling range.

The dumbass had either forgotten about her knives or was so enraged, he didn't care. Zadia got one of her hands between them, stabbing him in the gut. He grunted but didn't stop pulling her against him. His eyes were bright and feverish as one hand grabbed her neck. His fingers were so long they easily spanned the length, and Zadia had a moment to wonder if she'd miscalculated. He might be strong enough to snap her neck with one hand...

Her other knife was still out and free. As he cut off her airways, squeezing her throat tightly, her arm wrapped around him, and she slammed her second knife into his lower back, aiming for the kidney. An anguished howl of pain erupted, and his grip on her neck tightened. Zadia struggled, wrapped in one of his arms, the other hand squeezing the hell out of her throat. Her lungs burned from the lack of air, and panic began to rise.

Why the hell wasn't he weakening?

Black spots were beginning to dance in front of her vision... then he slumped, and his grip loosened.

Zadia gasped for air as he finally toppled to the ground. Fuck, that had taken longer than it should have.

No... correction—longer than she'd thought it would. The Warguard weren't the only ones getting over-confident. She should have never let him pull her in so close. Shaking her head in disgust at herself, Zadia glanced around the street as she re-sheathed her knives and rubbed her throat.

The street remained quiet and empty, but she was sure there were eyes watching.

Movement caught her eye, and she turned to look, moving into a battle-ready stance... but it was the Beta female they'd rescued, timidly moving toward her and holding out her hands in front of her, something glinting in them. Marcus and Vin's knives, recovered from the two dead guards.

She really was a brave Beta, retrieving those and following Zadia to return them. Zadia did her best to smile rather than grimace as she approached the frightened female.

"Thank you," the Beta said, handing the knives to Zadia before turning and darting away.

"Get inside, somewhere safe!" Zadia called after her. "And if anyone asks, Malachi sent us!" She was loud enough, anyone in the surrounding buildings should have heard. It wasn't the first time she'd said something similar today, and she doubted it would be the last.

Malachi's name would be on everyone's lips in the Warlord's territory tonight.

GRIGORI

The stench of Omega and Alpha fluids reeked so strongly, Grigori could smell it from the end of the hall. His lip curled. He would not be reporting to Malachi right now; no one would. Anger burned in his gut, knowing Tatiana had submitted to the Alpha's lust once again.

Pressing his lips together, he skirted the hall, back toward the room where Jeffos' son was resting. It had been hours, so perhaps the whelp had awoken while he was gone.

Jeffos was put out by his son's survival, which was almost enough to make Grigori want to congratulate Malachi on such an inspired act. Almost. Word in the kitchens was the unfortunate Omega who Jeffos had rutted today had survived the ordeal, barely. He was in a foul mood.

That some of his Warguard had been found dead in the street wasn't going to help matters. Grigori would need to go out again tomorrow to find out what Jeffos' reaction to *that* was.

Approaching the room where the Warlord's son was resting, he heard voices, including Cora's. Rather than going into the room and facing her again, Grigori paused for a moment, then changed direction, heading for the room next to it. With a glass to the wall, he would be able to hear what they were saying well enough. He didn't recognize one of the voices, which could only mean one thing.

The Warlord's son was awake.

7

THE SON AWAKENS

Jordan

Everything hurt. Which could only mean one thing—he wasn't dead. Considering how he felt, he wasn't sure that was actually a good thing. Every breath he took was a sharp jab of pain right through his center. When he tried to open his eyes, it was like ice picks stabbing into him, and he cried out. He barely made an audible sound, but the pain of the attempt was so much, he nearly blacked out.

Wished he had blacked out.

Then he wouldn't hurt so much.

"Relax. Breathe. Shallow breaths." The voice was female. Commanding. His instincts were riled, knowing another Alpha was ordering him what to do, but his brain was working enough to know she was right. She was trying to help.

Just like the green-eyed stranger in the street who had saved his life.

Malachi.

An unusual name and not one Jordan had heard before.

As his labored breathing slowed, he heard other sounds. The soft sound of fabric brushing against itself, next to him where the female's voice had come from and from across the room where someone else must be standing. He tried to breathe in through his nose, looking for a scent, but it was blocked. The memory of it breaking drifted through his mind.

"Where am I?" His voice was a hoarse whisper. "Who are you?" Was Malachi there? The Alpha he'd sworn himself to?

"My name is Cora. You are in the Riversong Territory. My territory."

He'd heard her name before. His muscles tensed, shooting more pain through him before he went limp with a groan. Fuck, that hurt. Riversong Territory. Such a pretty name for such a deadly place. It bordered his father's territory, Jeffos' Territory. Arrogant bastard had never given its own name. It was just his. Jeffos had plans for Riversong and Cora.

A small chuckle rasped from Jordan's throat.

"Is something funny?" Her voice was light, but there was a warning. From everything Jordan had heard, she was not an Alpha to be taken lightly. He also guessed her co-Alpha, Trace, was the other one in the room. Rumor said she rarely went anywhere without him, and the two of them preferred to share Omegas rather than claim their own. Jeffos had sneered at the idea.

"I was hoping to contact you." That had been part of his plan to overthrow his father. For all Jeffos' scorn about a female Alpha led territory, he'd also feared Cora. Jordan had been able to tell.

"Well, here I am." A spark of amusement and curiosity threaded through her tone.

Jordan dared to open his eyes again. The light in the room still hurt, but it was bearable, more like needles prickling his eyeballs instead of stabbing through them straight into his brain. He blinked several times as his vision cleared.

Movement in the corner of his eye turned into an Alpha female staring down at him. She was beautiful—medium brown skin and dark brown eyes full of sharp intelligence. A multitude of braids were pulled back from her face, pouring over her shoulders, decorated with beads at the end.

He went still, knowing how vulnerable he was with her looming over him. The smile she bestowed on him as they studied each other was not particularly reassuring.

"Do you know Malachi?" he asked, not wanting to discuss why he'd hoped to contact her before he understood more about his current situation. That he wasn't dead was already a surprise. Now he wanted to assess his circumstances before making any rash decisions. He'd already made one by pledging himself to a male he knew nothing about.

"Yes." Cora's full lips curved into a smile. "He's one of my allies. I'm helping him overthrow your father."

CORA

Interesting. An expression lit up Jeffos' son's expression at her declaration, but it wasn't fear, anger, or denial. With his battered, swollen features, it was hard to tell what it was, but if she was pressed to describe it, she would say excitement lit up his icy blue eyes. Perhaps even hope.

Very interesting.

She'd been more than a little dubious when Malachi brought the young Alpha here. Malachi's headquarters weren't so much in Riversong Territory as in the no-man's-land border between Riversong and Jeffos' territories, though it was closer to Riversong. The streets of that border were full of uninhabited and crumbling buildings that formed a buffer.

A buffer Jeffos had been testing more and more over the past few years, which was why she'd aligned herself with Malachi when he approached her. She hated Jeffos. Having someone as a neighbor who wasn't constantly looking to encroach into her territory would be a relief, especially when there had been some rumblings from Zone 1 recently.

"Malachi wants to overthrow my father?" Despite the raspy, hoarse quality of his voice, Jordan's excitement and relief came through. The question also exhausted him, and he closed his eyes, his big body relaxing on the table. "I will do whatever I can to help."

"As revenge?" Cora was not unhappy to have a new ally, especially an insider to the Warlord's circles, but she didn't trust easily. Especially not those who were from the enemies' encampment. Over her shoulder, she sensed Trace stirring, sliding closer. He was interested in the young Alpha's answer.

"Yes, but not for this." His face twitched. Anger? Hate? Her nostrils flared. Under the blood and the pain, she could smell his rage. "He could have saved my mother, but he let her die. Tossed her into the street like trash when she got the blood fever. I've been waiting years to take him down."

Blood fever. Deadly but curable with treatment. It would have been expensive for anyone but Jeffos. Cora doubted he would have even noticed the dent in his coffers. She was not surprised he hadn't provided it. Jeffos did not have a reputation for treating his Omegas well.

That was why Malachi had set himself against Jeffos. He and Jeffos' son had that in common. It was almost karmic retribution that the two of them would find each other and bring about Jeffos' downfall. What happened afterward would be interesting. She knew Malachi intended to rule the territory, taking Jeffos' place, but what about Jeffos' son?

"Did you intend to take his place?"

There was a long moment of silence. Cora waited patiently, watching every minute change in his expression and body language. Trace came up beside her to do the same. They would compare notes later, the way they always did. He liked her to take the lead so he could watch everyone and everything, and he always picked up on things she didn't.

To her, it didn't look as though Jordan was trying to decide whether to be truthful or making a new decision because of Malachi's plans. It was as if she'd asked him a question he'd never asked himself. One he hadn't thought of. Cora hoped she was wrong because if she was right, it didn't say much about his intelligence.

He'd been seeking to overthrow his father but hadn't thought about what would happen after? She'd better be wrong.

"I don't know," he said finally. Inwardly, Cora sighed. "I don't think I truly expected it to work, or I thought I'd be dead by the end of it, but I had to try."

Ah. Not entirely stupid, then. Cynical. And probably a realist.

Eyes still closed, he looked incredibly young lying there. Cora was only about a decade older, but she had clawed her way up through the Riversong Territory by the time she was twenty-two. Only a few years older than he was now. By the time he was her age, he'd be a force to be reckoned with… if he lived through it.

She exchanged glances with Trace. He nodded. They didn't need to speak to know they both felt Jordan was telling the truth—and Trace approved of his outlook. Trace would. He was a consummate realist.

Noises in the hall indicated someone was coming closer, and Trace immediately slipped back into position against the wall. Jordan's eyes flew open, his instincts telling him to get to his feet. Cora reached out and put her hand on his forehead, holding him down. She didn't think she could touch anywhere else without causing him more pain, which would make his instincts harder to fight.

"Hush. It's just Malachi and Tatiana."

"Tatiana?"

"Malachi's Omega." Though she remained unclaimed, that was who she was. Cora didn't blame Malachi for holding off on that final step. Trace's and her situation was different. Eventually, they might find an Omega to share permanently or Omegas for them to claim on their own, but right now, to do so would put that Omega in far too much danger. Omegas weren't completely helpless, but when it came to a fight, they were more easily overpowered by the Alphas than the Betas were. Their instincts told them to submit.

Tatiana was Malachi's greatest weakness, and they all knew it.

A moment later, the couple strode into the room. Tatiana darted over to Jordan, going into her healer-mode, much to Malachi's obvious chagrin—though he did not stop her once he saw Cora standing beside Jordan. He knew Tatiana was in no danger with Cora there, no matter what Jordan might try.

"How do you feel? Does your head hurt?" Tatiana's fingers pressed lightly against Jordan's temples, and the young Alpha groaned.

Something flashed in Malachi's eyes. Cora smirked at him. Watching him deal with Tatiana's caretaking of other Alphas was always amusing.

"Is he up to talking?" Malachi asked, striding to the other side of the table, standing beside Tatiana. His hand moved, and Cora knew he was resting it on the Omega's back, staking his claim while she tended to Jordan.

"We've been getting to know each other." Cora cocked her head and raised her eyebrow at Malachi, wondering what his plan was now. He would have one in his head, he always did, even if he didn't share it—which was often. Part of the reason Cora had stayed to watch over Jeffos' son was curiosity about Jordan, but the other was curiosity about what Malachi wanted him for.

"I can speak for myself," Jordan rasped, turning his head slightly and wincing at even that small movement.

Angling himself so he could look down at the young Alpha, Malachi's green eyes were calm. Controlled. Giving nothing away.

"Good. Now, tell me why I shouldn't kill you."

8

THE DEATH BARGAIN

Tatiana

"Give me a reason not to kill you."

Malachi's demand stiffened Tatiana's spine.

Had Malachi really just ordered her patient to give a reason not to execute him? That's what it would be—an execution. He was in no condition to fight back. She would be pissed if Malachi undid all the hard work she'd put into saving the young Alpha's life. Especially if Malachi didn't have a good reason—and being Jeffos' son wasn't a good reason. No one chose their parents.

Oddly, the Warlord's son did not appear at all disturbed by the threat.

"Seems like it would be a waste of saving me." A small smile quirked his lips before pain flashed in his blue eyes again. So young and so cynical. Then again, considering Jeffos had tried to have him executed, she could only imagine what growing up had been like for the young Alpha.

Malachi chuckled, and Tatiana rolled her eyes. More Alpha posturing. She should have realized. Malachi's hand slid up from her back to the back of her neck, his thumb stroking over her pulse, and she sighed, relaxing. Even though he hadn't been able to see her face, she was sure he knew she'd rolled her eyes.

His touch made her throb all over again, despite the satisfaction they'd already found together today. It wasn't unusual, but the force of it made her think she must be approaching another heat cycle soon. Blast. They didn't have time for that, but she couldn't stop it. In fact, the pleasurable interlude might have even moved things along.

For the first time since she'd met Malachi, the suppressors Grigori always tried to convince her would be salvation didn't sound like such a bad idea. She didn't want to be a distraction for him, but she also knew Malachi would never allow it. He hated the very idea of suppressors and life in the Zones.

"Very true." Malachi gave Tatiana's neck one last caress, then half sat on the table where Jordan was lying, looking down at him. "Why was the Warguard beating you to death?"

The young Alpha bared his teeth.

"They didn't say, but I can only assume it's because my father discovered my connection to the Underground."

Everyone in the room seemed to stop breathing. Malachi blinked, and Tatiana could practically hear his thoughts racing.

"It exists?" she asked tentatively. Jordan's gaze tore away from Malachi's blank expression and flickered over to her. While they'd heard of the Underground—the shadowy group working to oppose Jeffos from within his own territories—Cora and Malachi had given it up as nothing more than a rumor. They hadn't been able to find a trace of a single member until now. At one point, Malachi had even dismissed it as probably being the work of a single person.

"It does. There aren't many of us, but we've been effectively driving my father to rage on a regular basis." Satisfaction flashed across his face.

"How many are you? How do you communicate? Can you get in touch with them from here?" Malachi's questions came rapid-fire, and Tatiana knew he was already adjusting his plans in his head to fit this new information. He used every tool at his disposal, and this would be no different.

"It would help if I knew exactly where 'here' is," Jordan said dryly, making Cora snort with amusement. It was hard not to admire his bravado, considering he was flat on his back and surrounded by strange Alphas. He wasn't letting Malachi push him around and still had a sense of humor, which made Tatiana like him even more. "Cora told me we're in Riversong Territory, but that covers a lot of ground."

"We're more in the no-man's-land between Riversong and Jeffos," Cora admitted after exchanging a quick glance with Malachi. "Toward the North end."

Jordan's eyebrows rose before his expression settled again. "That's awfully close to Jeffos' palace."

"Which means it's unexpected." Malachi grinned.

"Very true." Jordan thought for a moment. "There's a drop-off point not far from no-man's-land, but I don't know if I could make it there right now."

"Could you describe it to us?" Malachi's voice was calm, even, but Tatiana knew him well enough to know he was excited. A connection to the Underground could only help them.

Instead of answering right away, Jordan hesitated.

"What do you want to say to them?" he asked.

"I want to offer an alliance and my help," Malachi said promptly. "And ask for their help. Do you know who their leader is?"

"We don't really have one." Jordan shrugged. Winced. Tatiana bit her lip. He needed to stop moving so much, but she knew it would be difficult. As injured as he was, there really wasn't much he could do without pain. "I'm not sure I know everyone involved. It's safest that way. We only meet up if someone needs help, and even then, a lot of them wear masks and scent-blockers and take other measures to hide their identities."

Malachi and Cora exchanged another glance.

Before they could start questioning Jordan again, a noise outside the door, followed by knocking, interrupted them.

"Come in," Cora called out.

Zadia entered a moment later with her Betas, Vin and Marcus, following behind. Marcus had his arm around a Beta female, who looked both worried and frightened. All of them were dusty and bloodied.

"Are you all alright?" Tatiana jumped forward, hands outstretched. "Where are you injured?"

Both Vin and Marcus fell back as Malachi's growl ripped through the room. The beta female looked as if she was about to turn and run. Only Zadia withstood the force of his displeasure, though her head bowed.

Turning, Tatiana put one hand on her hip and pointed her other finger at him.

"Stop that right now. I need to check to see if they're injured."

Malachi's green eyes flashed as he got to his feet, coming toward her. Her heart jumped in her chest, and she ducked her head. His arms wrapped around her, and he inhaled, breathing in her scent. She relaxed against his broad chest, doing the same.

"Next time, move slower. Please." The 'please' was tacked on as an afterthought. It was more of an order than a request, but she knew he was trying. Truthfully, he gave her so much more leeway than most Alphas gave Omegas. His possessiveness was instinctual, and sometimes, she forgot.

Being held by him, her senses stirred again, and he stiffened against her. If she was feeling the first inklings of her heat, he could likely scent it, which would not help, either.

"Sorry," she murmured. "I'll be good."

Lips pressed against her head, then he turned her around, releasing her.

The Beta female still looked frightened but also intrigued. Tatiana started patching them all up. Thankfully, none of them were badly injured, though Zadia's bruised throat was made Tatiana 'tsk' over it. As she looked them over, they reported in. The Beta female was introduced as Adriana, and she clung to Vin, who kept his arm around her.

Aw. That was sweet.

Thankfully, the female wasn't badly hurt, just a few bruises and scratches from the Warguard. They hadn't had time to do more than shove her around. God, Tatiana hated them. She pushed those feelings to the side as she worked. They weren't helpful.

"They're searching everywhere for him and making examples out of anyone who dares stand up to them or walks across the street at the wrong time," Zadia said, glancing at Jordan. "Hearing he escaped seems to have emboldened some of the territory's population, and they're mostly paying for it with their lives. We saved some of them, and they'll remember Malachi's name."

"They need something, someone, to rally around," Adriana murmured, then blushed when everyone looked at her, her eyes dropping to the ground.

"You're saying there are those in Jeffos' territory who are ready to rise up against him?" Malachi asked gently. Tatiana knew he and Cora had many talks about that exact idea. It was what they were hoping for, but they weren't certain of it. The rumors of the Underground had given them more hope, but they hadn't been sure of that, either.

Adriana was a regular Beta, so if she felt that way, if she thought the territories' population was looking for a leader, it was a promising sign. Hope rose in Tatiana as Adriana nodded.

"Those who confronted the Warguard today, they were the most foolish and the bravest, but there are many who are quieter but just as determined. Willing to wait for the right moment. For someone to follow." Adriana's voice grew stronger as though she was trying to convince Malachi. Tatiana could have told her he would need no coaxing to step up as the savior of Jeffos' Territory. "For a long time, his Warguard terrified everyone into submission, but he miscalculated. Been too selfish. Too brutal. People don't want to submit to his selfish rules anymore, and they are willing to fight for that change."

As if her words buoyed Malachi up, filling him, his chest swelled. If his green eyes had been glowing before, that was nothing compared to how bright they were now, like a flame had been lit from within.

"My name is Malachi," he told her. "And that is exactly what I intend to do." Abruptly he turned, refocusing on Jordan, who was still lying on the table, listening.

"Jeffos' son," he said. Behind him, Adriana gasped, but Malachi ignored her. Tatiana's heart pounded again. She knew what was happening in this room right now would be the beginning or the end of all of them. "Will you help me lay some bait for Jeffos?"

Jordan snorted. "I presume I'm the bait?"

"Once you can walk." Malachi glanced at Tatiana. She scowled at him, but she understood.

"He should be able to walk in a few days," she said reluctantly. "But he won't be able to fight."

"All he'll need to do is walk." Malachi patted Jordan's leg. "Do not worry, son of Jeffos, I am not about to sacrifice your life so quickly."

"Even if you did, it would not matter, as long as you promise to kill Jeffos." Jordan's eyes were bleak. So young and so lacking in hope for the future. Tatiana wanted to give him a hug, but she knew Malachi would never allow it, even if he wasn't feeling particularly possessive right now.

"I promise."

Jordan lifted his hand, and Malachi gently gripped it, sealing his promise.

On the rooftop, a shadow flitted away into the growing dark of the evening.

9

MALACHI'S ANGEL

Grigori

Lying on his back, staring up at the stars, Grigori did not know how to feel.

He hated Malachi and wanted him to die. But Malachi was marginally better than Jeffos. The lesser of two evils. Grigori sneered. Perhaps they would do him a favor and take each other out.

He wished Tatiana would come with him to the Zones. Or that he could get his hands on some suppressors... He'd asked the last time he'd gone to Zone One with information, but they'd told him his information wasn't useful enough yet.

Soon, he promised himself.

Soon he would have everything he wanted, then he could show Tatiana how much better life could be.

Tatiana

Following Adriana and Vin through the streets, Tatiana's heart was pounding. She had not been back in Jeffos' territory since she'd nearly been taken to be part of his harem. Now she was not only back by choice, she knew her heat was coming soon. Not yet, but her scent had thickened, and soon the instinct to build a nest would become overpowering.

In the meantime, she was determined to help.

Glancing at the huge Alpha beside her, she felt a little reassured. Malachi emanated menace. One hand on her lower back, the other flexing at his side, his head was moving back and forth, constantly on watch.

Zadia and Marcus brought up the rear, just as watchful and wary.

Convincing Malachi to let her come help those who had been injured by the Warguard had been an argument and a half, but Tatiana hadn't backed down. She'd finally won him over by pointing out this would be another way he could help. Word would spread, not only his name and that his people had fought back against the Warguard—and won—but he'd come to provide aid in their wake.

It was a very good argument, but he still hadn't wanted to give in. He'd allowed himself to be persuaded—eventually—but only if he came with her, which she'd then argued against.

The risk was high for all of them, but if word he was in Jeffos' territory reached the Warguard, after today's events, Tatiana had no doubt the Warlord would strike with overwhelming force. As an unmated Omega, her life was safe enough, at least for a while, even if she was captured. Wasn't that the whole point of remaining unmated?

Malachi had won the argument, eventually. Tatiana had known he would, though she'd hoped he'd see reason. Perhaps if she hadn't been so close to her heat, he would have.

Looking over her shoulder, Adriana waved at them, gesturing them toward the shadows, before running up to a door and knocking. A moment later, someone answered. From where Tatiana was huddled, between a wall and Malachi's muscled frame, she couldn't see who Adriana was talking to. It was a bit nerve-wracking. She didn't think Adriana would betray them, but it would be so, so easy.

After a long moment, Adriana turned and beckoned them.

Hand on Tatiana's back, Malachi led her forward, head still

swiveling back and forth even though there was no sign of anyone else on the darkened street. The Warguard was probably patrolling, but so far, they hadn't seen hide nor hair of them. Tatiana hoped it stayed that way.

"This is Malachi," Adriana said as they approached, with Zadia and Marcus following. By agreement, Tatiana was not to be introduced, her name going unmentioned, but it was minor protection. The Beta male Adriana was talking to stared at Tatiana, drawn in by her scent as much as her diminutive stature, the combination marking her as an Omega. Malachi growled, and the Beta's gaze immediately changed course, meeting Malachi's green eyes. He gulped, and Adriana continued soothingly. "He is here to help."

"You have injured?" Malachi asked, his deep voice rolling out with his most charming tone as if he hadn't just growled at the Beta. The Beta nodded, his jaw tightening.

"My younger brother, he... he threw a rock at the Warguard. He's only fourteen."

Tatiana sucked in a breath. Young and dumb, but oh so brave.

"Let me see him," she demanded.

The Beta kept his gaze averted from her as he nodded and turned, leading them into the dwelling. Malachi walked in front of her, Zadia directly behind her, keeping her safe from every direction, even though there was no threat. They passed through the main room, down a hallway to a bedroom. Even from the hall, she could smell the blood and pain. Knowing it belonged to a child... Her heart constricted. She hated Jeffos and his asshole Warguards so much.

In the bedroom, a woman knelt by the bed, holding the hand of the slender youth lying on it, quietly sobbing.

Clenching her jaw when she saw him, Tatiana pushed back her own tears. He truly was nothing more than a child, and they'd beaten him almost as badly as they had Jordan, then left him, knowing he would likely die of his injuries.

Not today.

Pressing her lips together, Tatiana went to her knees beside the boy, setting her bag on the floor and opening it. Adriana knelt beside her, holding and whispering to the child's mother. Behind her, Zadia spoke to the older brother in a low tone.

Tatiana ignored them all. She had work to do.

GRIGORI

Whispers were spreading on the wind by dawn.

Malachi had come into Jeffos' territory with an Angel. That's what they called Tatiana. It had to be her. Jeffos' people didn't say "Omega," they called her Malachi's Angel.

They had come in the dark of night and brought the gift of healing.

Despite it being a measure of protection for her, even that made Grigori's rage surge. She was *his* Angel, dammit.

He pushed down his anger. This, too, was something he could use.

He made his way back to Malachi's base, stopping here and there to speak with those whispering. Many of them knew him or had seen him. All of them were solemnly exchanging information, urging the secrecy. No one wanted a repeat of yesterday, and now they had something to help sustain them as they awaited Malachi's next move —hope.

Back in the building, Grigori hurried through the halls until he found Malachi, Cora, and Trace in one of the meeting rooms. The female Alpha's upper lip lifted in a threatening sneer when he entered, but he ignored her.

Malachi's green gaze caught his.

"Jeffos' territory is filled with your name, and word is spreading that your 'Angel' healed quite a few dissenters last night," Grigori said bluntly. Cora might not like him, but even she couldn't deny he was useful—something he endeavored to be so she couldn't convince Malachi to cut him loose.

"My Angel?" Malachi's lips twitched as though he almost smiled. Hate seethed in Grigori's gut, but he pushed it down, hiding it. He never wanted Malachi to know how much he loathed him. While he was sure Malachi knew Grigori disliked him, he didn't think the Alpha had any idea the depths to which that dislike plummeted. "That is very fitting. Nothing about her being an Omega?"

The note of concern in his voice made Grigori want to slap him. If he was so concerned about Tatiana's safety, he shouldn't have brought her into Jeffos' territory in the first place, but no, he hadn't been able to miss a chance to show off how wonderful he was and use Tatiana to do it.

Poor fuckers. They thought they'd be getting an upgrade with Malachi, but he was the same wolf in sheep's clothing, just far more subtle. Oh, well, if they fell for Malachi's bullshit, that was their problem. Grigori could only do so much. He couldn't spend his time worrying about a bunch of random Betas who chose to follow Alpha assholes. They could be like him and try to get into the Zones, but they stayed here, drudging away for the Alphas.

"Nothing," Grigori confirmed, keeping his tone even. Light. "So far, it doesn't seem word has spread to the Warguard. They do not appear to know you were in the territory last night."

Thankfully. That would have put Tatiana in even more danger. Not to mention all the people she'd helped. Had Malachi thought about that? If Jeffos found out Malachi had been there, helping people, all the people he'd helped would be in more danger. It wouldn't surprise Grigori if Malachi hoped for such an outcome. Jeffos would bring his boot down harder, which would make the citizens of his territory want him gone even more. Now, Malachi had given them the hope of something different. Someone new.

Blatant manipulation and propaganda—that's what it was. Which was why no Alpha could be trusted. Malachi was setting himself up to be better than Jeffos, to make everyone think he was, but he was just more of the same.

Selfish. Egotistical. Power-hungry.

"Good. Thank you, Grigori." Malachi dismissed him with a nod, looking at the papers on the table in front of him, and rage surged through Grigori.

The dismissive, paltry gratitude was far less than he deserved. He hadn't had to come to Malachi. Clenching his jaw, ignoring Cora's dark-eyed glare, he spun on his heel and stalked back out.

It felt like that was all he was doing lately—stalking in and out of Malachi's compound.

He headed in a different direction until he reached his own hidden base, the one he'd carved out for himself not long after Malachi had found him and Tatiana. There was a comm unit there, hidden under a loose floorboard and wrapped in rags.

Pulling it out, he turned it on and pressed the red button on the side, sending the signal he was there and available to talk. He did not have long to wait before it beeped back at him.

"Checkmate," he said, giving the code word to indicate it was him, and he was alone.

"Report."

Grigori quickly summarized the events of the past few days, everything from finding the Warlord's son to Tatiana's new designation as Malachi's Angel. There was silence on the other end, but he knew they were taking in every word.

"I want the suppressors now," he said after he finished. "I want suppressors and a safe space for Tatiana and me in the Zone."

"You have not given us enough information yet. We still need you there, which means she needs to stay there as well."

Grigori gritted his teeth. "What more could you possibly need? This war is about to erupt."

"Let me know when Malachi is actually going to challenge the Warlord, not that it's coming soon, but the actual day. Then we'll talk."

Pressing his lips together, Grigori ended the transmission without acknowledgment. Bastard.

Grigori didn't have any other choice except to deal with him... for now.

10

PLANS & CONFESSIONS

Jordan

The Omega smelled delicious. No matter his wounds, his body reacted as Tatiana replaced his bandages. Behind her, Malachi growled threateningly, scenting Jordan's involuntary reaction.

He responded by keeping his eyes firmly closed, staying perfectly still, and doing his best to think about something else. Anything else. Like how much he still hurt. The look on Morpheus' face when he'd thought he'd won. The loathing that churned Jordan's stomach whenever he had to be in his father's presence.

Nothing helped. His body still reacted. And so he held very, very still until Tatiana was done and her gentle fingers moved away. Only when she stepped back did he fully relax, no longer worried Malachi would rip out his throat for making the wrong move while Tatiana touched him.

The little Omega was going into heat. Jordan didn't blame Malachi for his protectiveness. An Omega in heat could make Alphas lose control, the instinct to rut overriding everything else. She wasn't there yet, but Malachi's and Jordan's instincts were telling them she would be soon. The urge was to sequester her away, where no other Alpha could find her, so he could rut and breed her when the time came—it didn't matter his injuries, the impulse was still there.

"Good. I think in about a week you should be able to move freely—"

"Two days." Malachi interrupted, and Tatiana gasped. Jordan opened his eyes, amused to see she had her hands on her hips and was glaring up at Malachi. She might be an Omega, but she certainly didn't act like the ones in Jeffos' harem.

"He won't be fully—"

"I don't need him fully healed," Malachi interrupted again, although he was looking at Jordan. Stepping forward, he didn't shoulder Tatiana aside, but he did put himself between her and Jordan. She made an exasperated noise from her new position behind him. "I need you mobile. In two days, I want to send you out into the Wastelands... temporarily."

Tatiana gasped with outrage, but Jordan got what Malachi was saying.

"You want my father to think I escaped out there."

Not that it would be much of an escape. The Wastelands were basically uninhabitable. Jeffos amused himself by banishing someone there rather than executing them. He found the idea of them slowly dying but still hoping they might find a way to live in that inhospitable barren land to be a more fitting punishment than a quick death.

"I want your father to think you found no refuge in Riversong and were forced to flee into the Wastelands. For that to be believable, you can't be fully healed, and we need to do this as quickly as possible."

"How long will I need to stay there?" Tension tightened his stomach. He'd thought he'd accepted his inevitable death at Morpheus' hands, but now that he'd been saved, he wanted to live. He wanted to kill Morpheus and his father or at the very least, witness their downfall.

"Not long. Zadia and her team will meet you out there with supplies. You will camp with them for several days before making your way back."

"Leaving Jeffos thinking I'm dead." There was a certain satisfaction in that idea. His father would never know what hit him. Jordan was determined to look him in the eye one last time before Jeffos died. Seeing his father's realization Jordan was still alive would be the icing on the cake.

"Exactly." Malachi's jade gaze swept over Jordan's prone figure. "Once that is done, we'll continue to make plans, but for now, I don't want Jeffos to think we got any information from you about him."

That made sense. Jordan made a face as he tried to move his legs. Pain throbbed through his side, and he sucked in a breath.

"Stop." Malachi put his hand on Jordan's shoulder. "Rest. You can try moving some tomorrow."

"He'll barely be able to walk in two days," Tatiana muttered behind him. Jordan could see her crossing her arms, a sulky expression on her beautiful face. An unfamiliar emotion trickled through him, warming him from the inside. He wasn't used to having someone care about what happened to him, not since his mother's death.

"Barely will be enough. We can wait three if we need to, but the sooner you're able, the more convincing it will be."

Jordan nodded, ignoring how the movement made it feel as if someone had just shoved an ice pick behind his eyes.

"I'll be ready."

CORA

Standing in her room overlooking her territory, Cora's dark eyes were drawn across the streets to where no man's land and Malachi were.

"Brooding again?" Trace's deep voice rumbled as he approached.

Cora snorted. "I'm not brooding. I'm thinking." Truthfully, she was doing both. There were times she questioned her alliance with Malachi, though she would choose him over Jeffos every day of the week, which was why she helped him.

She also knew how powerful an Alpha he was. With a territory of his own...

She had to trust their alliance would hold, and Malachi wouldn't turn into another power-hungry bastard like Jeffos. There was only so much territory one Alpha could hold and suitably lead, something Jeffos had never understood because as far as Cora could tell, he didn't care about those living under his rule. He just wanted more. There was no quenching his appetite—not for power, land, or cruelty. In fact, the more he got of the first two, the more he indulged in the third.

"You are doing both," Trace echoed her thoughts as he came to stand by her side. His big hand curved around her hip, stroking and stirring her senses. It wasn't the same as when they had an Omega to share—it never was—but Trace was her soulmate in every other sense of the word, and her desire flared as he caressed her.

Turning, Cora tilted her head back and reached up to pull him down for a kiss. There was a momentary hesitation—there always was, not because he didn't want to kiss her but his instincts demanded he be the one to take charge, not give in to her—but he wanted to kiss her, and that desire overrode his instincts.

Their mouths met, fused with a passion others might describe as angry. It wasn't, but it wasn't soft either. It wasn't tender. Their passion always began with a battle for dominance, their Alpha instincts pushing to the fore and demanding supremacy over the other. Though he submitted to her leadership outside of the bedroom, within it, they were constantly contending for superiority.

Cora raked her nails across the back of his neck, eliciting a growl. He grabbed her long braids with one hand, using them to pull her head backward, breaking the kiss, so he could go for her throat. Hot, wet kisses accompanied a scrape of teeth over tender skin, and she hissed at the sensation.

They moved as one, tearing at each other's clothes, leaving a trail of fabric and leather from the window to the bed.

"What did you want?" She pushed him down onto his back. It didn't matter that he was bigger than her, she could still overpower him. His body might be larger and more muscular, but she was faster and knew exactly where to put her hands on his body to get the reactions she wanted. Trace's eyes flashed, and he bared his teeth, a gleaming white threat on his dark face.

"Malachi wants to meet with us again next week."

He attempted to roll, to put her beneath him, but Cora twisted, her hands down on his collarbone and her hips lining up with his. The thick head of his cock found her slick opening, and she sank onto him.

Groaning, Trace's lower body surged upward, thrusting into her hard and fast. Filling his hands with her hanging breasts, he pinched her nipples viciously in retaliation for being placed beneath her. Cora moaned, her inner muscles tightening around his thick girth as the pain and pleasure flashed through her, mingling together.

Sometimes, she cursed that Trace wasn't an Omega, that she couldn't bite and claim him the way she could an Omega, but at the same time, she loved him the way he was. Vicious and ruthless enough to match her, the passionate struggle between them keeping her on her toes.

Sliding one hand up to his throat, she squeezed lightly, feeling the vibration of his grunt against her palm as she rode him, using his thick cock for her pleasure while he squeezed and pinched her breasts in painful counternote to her growing ecstasy.

The knot at his base thickened, swelling, and she knew it pained him, which made her enjoyment heighten. Her body was not made to fit a knot, no matter how aroused she was, so she ground down atop it, rubbing her clit against the thick bulge every time she slid down his cock, tormenting him as she pleasured herself.

"Fuck! Cora!" His hips surged upward, impaling her. He groaned as he began to cum, and his handsome face twisted in the agony and ecstasy his orgasm triggered without the knot being engaged.

Cora took him as deep as she could, rubbing against the top of the knot, which she knew would provide him with some relief but not enough. The heady mix of pain and pleasure left them both fulfilled, yet unsatisfied, their bodies throbbing. They screamed their anger and passion at being the other's match, yet being made so they could never be enough for each other.

As they laid in the dark, bodies still entwined, still throbbing from needs unmet, Cora kissed his fingers where they wrapped around hers. They were not a tender couple, but as the inevitable war with Jeffos grew closer, she treasured these intimate moments even more.

"I love you, Trace," she whispered into the dark, words she never spoke aloud in the light of day for fear they would be seen as weakness.

A long moment passed, and her heart clenched. She wished she hadn't spoken. Then Trace pulled her closer, holding her tighter, and she felt his lips brush over the top of her braids.

"We are going to live through this, Cora." His voice was as soft as hers but firm in its belief. "We will defeat Jeffos, Malachi will take over his territory, then we will have peace."

"I know," she whispered. It was what she wanted. What they both wanted. What they had planned and prepared for.

Another long moment, where they did nothing more than hold each other, then Cora closed her eyes.

The sound was soft as down, barely audible, even to her senses as though Trace had breathed out the words without meaning to put voice to them.

"I love you, too."

11

THE OMEGA'S HEAT

Tatiana

Tatiana's stomach cramped so hard, she couldn't ignore it, though she might try. Wetness gushed into her underwear, sweet-smelling and slick. She whimpered as every head turned toward her, their eyes alight with aroused interest.

No, not now! The little voice in her mind that wailed was that of a frustrated woman, unable to control her own body.

They didn't have time for her to go into heat right now.

She'd been ignoring the signs, continuing as if she didn't feel the warning twinges in her belly, as though she could hold it off by a sheer force of will, but unfortunately, that had never been true.

Suppressors don't sound so bad now, do they?

Tatiana didn't like the idea, didn't like to think how in the Zones, people were denied their true nature—not everything about being an Omega was bad—but at moments like this, she longed for more control over herself.

Frustrated tears filled her eyes as Malachi stepped between her and Jordan, her body throbbing in reaction to his growl and the overwhelming scent of her Alpha... of multiple Alphas. She responded to Malachi the most because he was the closest and also the one she truly wanted. That was the curse of the Omega. If he wasn't there when she went into rut... She shuddered at the thought of being taken by an unknown Alpha or even a friend. The only one she'd ever wanted was Malachi.

Being claimed would change that, make it so the other Alphas would have less interest in her and she in them, but that wasn't an option right now. And even then, it wouldn't change that the only one she wanted was Malachi, it would only make that more true.

"We have to go." He turned her away from the bed. She'd been replacing Jordan's bandages, doing her best to give the young Alpha every chance when he was out in the Wastelands. Especially since he would first try to get the attention of the Warguard to make sure they saw him go.

It was going to be dangerous. He still wasn't fully healed.

"No, I can't." She pushed back, trying to turn back around, but it was fruitless. The moment she turned, Malachi tossed her over his shoulder as if she weighed nothing, carrying her from the room.

Tatiana's insides clenched, more slick pouring from her as the scent of Malachi surrounded her, his hands on her, his body pressed against hers, even though he was carrying her over his shoulder like a sack of potatoes.

The last thing she before the room closed was Zadia moving in to take over where Tatiana had to leave off. Zadia was good, but she wasn't at Tatiana's level.

She could scream with frustration, but she sagged over Malachi's shoulder. There was no point in fighting her nature or his.

"Good girl." His large hand palmed her bottom, and Tatiana moaned, shuddering. Another cramp twisted her stomach, making her whimper and cringe as the affected area bounced on his shoulder.

Malachi pulled her into a new position, cradled against his chest. Now she could see his glare of aggression at everyone who looked at them.

Alphas and Betas alike turned or backed away when they saw

Malachi. None of them were game to challenge him for the right to rut her... but he needed to go, too.

By the time he reached their room, Tatiana had made her decision.

"You have to go," she whispered. "I'll stay here."

"No." It was a simple, definitive statement. He put Tatiana on her feet, close to the bed. Glancing at it, she pushed down the urge to burrow in and tuck the sheets and blankets around her. It would feel so good and would help ease the instincts riding her.

But Malachi needed to go. He needed to make sure everything went according to plan with Jordan and the others.

"Go." She put her hands on her hips, doing her best to glare at him. "I will be fine until you can get back."

"No." Rather than wait for another argument, Malachi stepped forward, grabbing her hair, using it to pull her head back, and forcing her to lift her lips for him to claim with a kiss.

It was a rough kiss, a claiming kiss, one that was spurred as much by her heat as anything else. Malachi was always rougher when she was in heat as if he knew she needed it that way. Tatiana whimpered as he dominated her with nothing more than his hand and mouth, his body backing her toward the bed.

More wetness came out in a gush, the scent rising in the air, heady and seductive. Malachi growled again as his tongue twined with hers and his cock pressed against her stomach, huge, hard, and throbbing. Her body pulsed in response, her insides clenching emptily.

Take me. Fill me.

Trying to hold a rational thought was a losing battle. Her body demanded, and she caved.

The sound of tearing fabric rent the air.

Tatiana tumbled back onto the bed with Malachi's large body atop hers. His lips devoured hers, hands sliding up to cup her breasts, the head of his cock nestling between her legs. She moaned, legs wrapping around his hips, pushing against him, needing him inside of her.

She ached all over, her instincts overriding all other considerations now that they were here.

"Malachi!" she gasped his name when he moved his lips away from hers, his hips thrusting forward and splitting her open. It hurt gloriously, her muscles burning from the sudden stretch around his thick girth, and her fingers curved to dig into his shoulders. Slick coated him, pouring from her in a torrent as he pumped inside her, driving away the sharpest pains of her need.

He pinched her nipples as his mouth moved to her neck, and she arched her head back, presenting her throat to him. A low growl vibrated through his large frame, and for a moment, she thought she had him, thought he might actually bite her.

He pulled away, and she wailed at the loss before he turned her onto all fours and slammed into her from behind. Her nails dug into the bed, toes curling, and she sobbed out a wild moan as Malachi pounded into her. Hands gripped her hips, pulling her back against him with every thrust, his knot growing and pushing at her, forcing her open.

His wild growls spurred her onward, her body clenching and writhing until ecstasy burst inside her. Fingers pressed down between the apex of her legs, rubbing against the swollen nub, and Tatiana screamed in passion as the sensations wracked her body.

The thick knot at the base of his cock pushed inside her, stretching her open so deliciously painful, and her muscles squeezed it hard, milking it of the thick ropes of seed her body craved. Completion was bliss, and Tatiana's tears fell to the mattress, her breath heaving in and out as Malachi shuddered atop her.

Her heat had impelled his rut, and his spend was thicker, hotter, filling her to the brim, his knot blocking its escape from her body. He flooded her womb while she clenched and quivered around him, a slave to her lusts and her need for him.

Malachi collapsed on top of her, his deep Alpha purr and the feel of his seed sloshing inside her, taking the edge off her body's demands. Tatiana panted beneath him, eyes half-closed, happily nestled between him and the mattress.

It wasn't long before her desire built again. She wiggled beneath him, bumping the curves of her buttocks back against his groin. His purr thickening and vibrating harder, he pulled out long enough to put her on her back. Tatiana reached for him, staring up at his broad chest, his dark hair dampened with sweat and curling around his brow.

He curved his arms over her legs, pressing her back into the bed, her knees bent and spread wide, so her swollen, leaking sex was completely vulnerable. She wriggled, whimpering and purring to coax him into her, and he did not wait.

Sliding into her, the combination of her slick and his cum lubricated her. Malachi thrust again, his green eyes glowing as he stared down at her.

Tatiana had forgotten all about Jordan and the plans to overthrow Jeffos. None of it mattered right now. Nothing mattered but the demands of her Omega instincts and the Alpha who was fulfilling them.

"Malachi!"

She screamed out his name, as she would over and over during her heat until she was hoarse and barely awake from exhaustion.

Jordan

Tatiana's absence was pure relief. The scent of her had been driving him wild, and ignoring it had been an exercise in pure frustration and willpower.

By the time Zadia finished bandaging him, Cora and Trace had come into the room to watch them. With a pinched expression, as if she was trying to hide her mistrust, Zadia helped Jordan to his feet.

He wasn't fully healed; he could feel that. Lying on his back had been easier than standing. At least he wasn't as bad off as he had been. Parts of him still ached, but it was tolerable, and the shakiness faded after a moment. He looked at Cora and Trace questioningly.

The female Alpha gave him a thin smile.

"With Malachi tending to Tatiana, Trace and I will help you get to the Wastelands and make sure some of the Warguard see you."

Jordan nodded his understanding, even as his brow crinkled.

"What?" Zadia asked, her voice harsh.

"It's just…" Jordan shrugged one shoulder. He shouldn't be surprised things were done differently here. "I know Malachi wanted to be here."

"He did, but none of us would ever leave an Omega in the kind of pain that an unsatisfied heat brings. Tatiana's needs come first. That's why we have multiple Alphas here, to lean on each other." Cora nodded at Zadia, who nodded back. Despite the fact Cora ruled her own territory and Zadia followed Malachi, the two of them were willing to work together to keep Tatiana from being in pain.

That was the biggest difference between them and Jeffos, Jordan realized. They would work together to help the weakest among them, whereas Jeffos had sometimes denied his Omegas an Alpha during their heat—if they'd displeased him or, occasionally, for his own entertainment, and sometimes, from pure indifference to their plight for there had been no Warguard that had impressed him enough to receive an Omega as a reward. He did not care that it was pure torture for the Omegas, as it did not affect him.

Nodding, Jordan felt his resolve grow again. He stood straighter, shoulders back. Malachi was the right Alpha to take over from his father. He would see Jeffos dead if it was the last thing he did, secure in the knowledge the territory would have a new, better leader.

"Let's go."

12

WRONG

Morpheus

Standing beside Jeffos, looking over the map of Jeffos' territory and what they'd been able to map out of Riversong's territory, Morpheus pointed out the places where they'd been looking for Jordan. The damned whelp. Thankfully, the territory had settled down since the day he'd gone missing. It had taken some demonstrations of how powerless the resident Betas were against the War Guard and a fair number of beatings, but the populace was back to being cowed.

No one had seen him since.

"He must have gone into Riversong. Or No Man's land. Or wherever this Malachi is from." Morpheus' nostrils flared. He had no doubt Jordan's disappearance and Malachi's appearance were connected, though he didn't think the males were one and the same. He thought it far more likely Malachi was the green-eyed Alpha who had rescued the whelp.

Jeffos disagreed.

"He is Malachi. There's no other explanation." Jeffos' crazed eyes gleamed. With every day that passed with no word of Jordan's location, he'd become more and more vicious.

Rather than argue, Morpheus kept his lips sealed. Jeffos didn't want to hear arguments, and at this point, he sure as hell couldn't prove his theory. Not until he had Jordan or the green-eyed Alpha in custody.

"Alpha!" The shout echoed through the chamber as one of Morpheus' men came bolting into the audience room. "Alpha, we've found him!" The guard was almost wild-eyed with glee, knowing he would be well rewarded for this report. "He was spotted in No Man's Land. It looks like Cora is sending him into the Wastelands."

"Well? Why didn't you bring him back with you?" Jeffos barked out.

The guard, whose name Morpheus was struggling and failing to remember, flushed, then paled.

"We attempted to, Alpha, but the Riversong soldiers fought us. He's still in their territory. They're sending him into the Wastelands, but they do not want us in their territory." The pleading note that had entered his voice made Morpheus want to snort. The male was not nearly as brave as he pretended. The Warguard was getting soft. He would have to do something about that. Maybe a culling of the weakest. Though the recent skirmishes with Malachi's forces had already begun that.

Still, a demonstration that weakness would receive no mercy at home would make for a good demonstration.

Morpheus eyed the guard, who had been happy to report Jordan's appearance in hopes of a reward but had failed to bring the whelp back. Perhaps they would start with him. He said nothing as Jeffos' attention turned to him. The Warlord was seething, his eyes full of fire.

"Go." The order was guttural. "This time, bring me his head."

There was no space for arguments.

Turning on his heel, Morpheus strode to the door, gesturing to the guard who had come in. *Chadrick.* That was his name. He had not stood out in Morpheus' mind because there was nothing to stand out about him. No wonder Morpheus had struggled to remember his name. He was an inferior Alpha.

"Show me."

As they exited into the compound, Morpheus gestured to several of the Alphas he trusted, guards who knew to gather their forces and head for the door. He would not empty the compound, but he intended to come with overwhelming force.

He did not like to think about what would happen if he failed.

GRIGORI

The Warlord's compound was emptying, yet quite a few remained. Grigori counted at least fifty Alphas heading into the streets. Far more than he knew Malachi, and the others had anticipated. It would likely be a slaughter.

For a long moment, he weighed what he preferred. By the time the doors shut behind the last of the Warguard following Morpheus, Grigori had started moving. He would warn Cora and Trace.

The decision would have been harder if Malachi had been with those sent to guard the Warlord's son and ensure he made it into the Wastelands. If Malachi was killed in a skirmish, everyone's hopes would dry up, and he might finally convince Tatiana to accompany him to Zone One. Though he wasn't sure his contact at Zone One would be happy since he wanted the disturbance outright war would bring.

It might have been worth it to be rid of Malachi.

Just thinking of the Alpha made Grigori's jaw hurt as he ground his teeth together, the muscle tightening to the point of pain. He relished it, leaning into it because it reminded him of why he was doing what he was doing. Free Tatiana of her base needs and the necessity of submitting to the Alpha's rut, so she could make her own choices instead of being a slave to her Omega nature.

One day, she'd have the suppressors. She'd be a Beta, like him, and would realize how much better off she was. She'd thank him, even though she didn't think it was what she wanted right now. When she understood, she would see how much better off she was with him instead of Malachi.

The Alpha wasn't doing his own dirty work, too busy indulging in the rut with Tatiana. He should have allowed another Alpha to take care of her, but no, Malachi was too selfish to share his Omega, even if he wouldn't claim her.

Running along the rooftop, he shimmied down the ladder on the other side and took off through the streets to where Cora and Trace were, right on the edge of No Man's land, waiting for the report for Zadia. Another fifteen Alphas and Betas were with them. Along with the five who had gone with Zadia, they would still be massively outnumbered.

They'd intended to catch some attention, but they hadn't expected Jeffos to empty his stronghold.

If they'd been more organized, they would have been able to hit the compound... instead, Cora's forces were still spread out through her own territory, along the boundaries, to keep Jeffos' Warguard at bay in case they attacked. They should have planned for this, but they were too stupid. They could have used Jordan as a distraction, rallied all those useless Betas they'd been sucking up to, and thrown them at the compound after it had been emptied.

Yes, the Betas would have been little more than cannon fodder, but they could have overwhelmed with their numbers, taken over the compound, then when Morpheus and the Warguard came back, they would have held the high ground. Apparently, no one thought of that or hadn't been willing to do it because of the sacrifice it would require from the Betas in Jeffos' zone... although they had already proven themselves willing to do so.

Eventually, Malachi would have to come down from his high horse if he wanted to actually defeat Jeffos.

Marek, one of the Alphas with Cora, lifted his head as Grigori hurried down the street. Grigori held back his own snarl. Of course, he had to choose the street where Marek was standing guard. Young, dumb, and aggressive, he would probably be killed in the coming war, and Grigori wouldn't shed a tear. He was so far up Cora's ass, it was a wonder Trace didn't object.

Crossing his arms over his chest as Grigori came running up, Marek frowned down at him.

"Move," Grigori snarled before Marek could open his mouth. "I need to talk to Cora and Trace."

Marek raised his dark eyebrows, uncrossing his arms and turning to his side, one hand coming out in a gesture of allowing Grigori to pass. He didn't bother speaking. Arrogant bastard. Grigori stalked past him, catching his breath.

At the center of the square, Cora and Trace were standing next to a table with maps laid out, comms in their ears. As he approached, they looked up. Cora frowned at him, straightening.

"Yes, Grigori?" And that was where Marek and the others got their arrogance. She couldn't even say his name without her tone dripping derision and disrespect. He would work with her and do his duty, anyway... for Tatiana.

"Morpheus has left Jeffos' stronghold with fifty warriors."

CORA

"Fifty?" Her jaw dropped open in shock. "That's more than half his forces!"

For Jeffos to send out so many, they'd hit his pride harder than she'd realized. For a moment, she wondered if they could rally enough soldiers to take the compound, but that would likely be a suicide mission and not one she would ask of her people. She and Malachi had discussed sending an assassin in after Jeffos if enough of his soldiers left to chase Jordan, but they'd ended up against the idea since they didn't have a trained assassin. Their people were trained to be soldiers.

Grigori would probably make a decent assassin, always sneaking around, getting into places he wasn't supposed to be, but Cora would never trust him enough. He would look out for his own interests, period, without a care for anyone else except maybe Tatiana.

Not the kind of person who she wanted to entrust with something as important as taking out Jeffos. He might decide at the last minute to switch sides. She didn't think he would while Tatiana was on the other side, but she could see his patience with that thinning by the day. Sometimes, she was surprised he hadn't already betrayed them.

She looked forward to ripping out his throat when he did. Right now, he was under Malachi's protection, but if he turned on them, that would end.

Until then...

"Fuck." Trace muttered, and Cora echoed the sentiment as they looked down at the maps. Zadia and the others would be massacred if they didn't move. Cora had been willing to keep Jeffos' men out of Riversong territory, but some of Malachi's plans would come to naught if Jordan and Zadia didn't make it into *and* out of the Wastelands.

She wished Malachi was here to make his own damn decision or at least for her to bargain with before she gave him her aid, but he was busy with Tatiana's heat. The Omega's needs came first.

Fuck.

Pressing her comms unit, she spoke into it.

"Zadia, the Warguard is coming for you, more than we expected. We're on our way with backup." Ha. Backup. They were still going to be outnumbered and outgunned. Heavily. Cora looked at Trace. His dark eyes were unfathomable as he looked back at her, his jaw clenched.

"First or second wave?" she asked. One of them needed to gather extra forces to backup to the backup if they were going to have a fighting chance. She and Malachi used mixed Alpha and Beta forces, unlike Jeffos, in part because most Alphas were swayed by the fact Jeffos had most of the Omegas in the area. They didn't care he'd obtained them through violence or that he didn't treat them properly.

The honorable Alphas belonged to her and Malachi, but unfortunately, there were fewer of them.

Their Betas were well trained but against an overwhelming Alpha force…

This had so many opportunities to go tits up.

"First…" Trace turned and barked orders. Immediately, their soldiers were on their feet, following behind him and falling into orderly ranks as they jogged down the street. Barely noticing Grigori at her side, Cora watched for a long moment, her chest tightening with worry as Trace left to gather up their extra forces.

She couldn't leave her own territory undefended, so she had to contact each unit one by one either to send one or two soldiers, wait for them to arrive, then head out to battle from here, hoping she would get there in time. She needed to stop thinking about what might happen if she didn't and get moving on contacting her units.

Getting back on the comms, changing the channel to the unit that was farthest away, she barely noticed as Grigori slipped away.

13

BATTLE & BLOOD

Zadia

Jogging through the streets, Zadia raised her knife in the air, letting loose a war cry.

"You'd better run, you coward! No surprise Jeffos' son is a weakling!"

So much for escorting Jordan into the Wastelands. With Cora's short, sharp warning—and lack of information about how many of the Warguard were in pursuit—Zadia made the decision to get them running. The faster they could get Jordan into the Wastelands, the better. The Warguard was unlikely to follow him out there. The Wastelands weren't kind, but Malachi regularly sent patrols out there to practice survival. Something they knew the Warguard didn't do.

Behind her, Vin and Marcus were hot on her heels. They were all doing their best to make it look like they were chasing Jordan, who was doing *his* best to run despite his wounds. She could smell his pain in the air as they followed, but he didn't falter. The Warlord's son was much more disciplined than any of his soldiers.

Suddenly, Marek burst out from one of the side streets, a snarl on his face, easily reaching Zadia's side.

"They're coming."

Fuck.

Picking up her pace, Zadia deliberately closed the distance between herself and Jordan, the other males right behind her. The rest of her team closed in on the sides. It looked as though they were closing Jordan in a pincer trap. Hopefully, there was no one watching from above who would notice it was taking far too long for the trap to close.

Then she heard them.

The pounding steps, the loud growls that rent the air.

Menace seemed to shimmer before her.

Despite everything, Zadia's heart seized with fear, her chest tightening as her instincts screamed *danger*.

She took the opportunity to slow, looking around, the rest of her soldiers doing so as well. Ahead of her, Jordan continued to forge ahead without looking back.

Right on the edge of Riversong territory, she snarled when she saw the Warguard coming down the street toward them. No-man's land was full of buildings, and they filled the street between the empty structures. Zadia felt her mouth dry—had the Warlord emptied his barracks? There was far, far more than she would have thought.

Time. I need to give Jordan time to get into the Wastelands.

Out of the corner of her eye, she could see another troop—Cora's soldiers—coming out of a street ahead, taking over his escort, leaving her and her team to face the Warguard, which was right and fair. Cora was sending backup. Zadia and her team, Malachi's people, would take the first wave of battle, and hopefully, the Warguard would think they were Riversong soldiers.

This was their fight, after all.

Morpheus

Seeing the small troop of Riversong soldiers ahead of him, just inside their territory, Morpheus narrowed his eyes. The whelp had just run past, right ahead of them. Were they there to kill the whelp or only drive him into the Wastelands? The latter was what Chadrick had made it sound like. He glanced over at the Alpha in question.

The weakling had paled at the sight of Riversong's warriors, even though Morpheus could tell half the troop were Betas rather than Alphas. He would ensure Chadrick didn't make it through the day. There was no place for weak Alphas in the Warguard.

"What are you doing here?" the female Alpha bitch called out to him. It figured Cora would have another Alpha bitch leading soldiers. Her dark hair was pulled up behind her head in a knot, and she was younger than Cora but very much like her. Morpheus' lip lifted in a sneer.

"We're here for the male you are chasing. Move out of our way, and we shall take him and leave."

The Alpha bitch scoffed, her voice carrying as she replied, filled with arrogance.

"Step one foot in our territory and die."

Now it was Morpheus' turn to scoff. She was posturing, surely. That or she had a death wish, which he would be happy to fulfill.

"We will crush you. Let us pass, and you will live. This is your last chance."

Frowning, the Alpha bitch ran her fingers over the knife belted to her hip. She looked as though she was thinking about it. Morpheus itched to run forward and teach her a lesson, but Jeffos did not want all-out war with Cora—not yet—and attacking her people in her own territory would instigate immediate retaliation.

He would do it, but if it wasn't necessary, it was best avoided.

Get the whelp, bring his head back to Jeffos, and reap the rewards without having to also report Cora would be retaliating for an attack.

The Alpha bitch bared her teeth. Stupid bitch. She was going to say no. He was looking forward to killing her.

"You cannot come in our territory. Follow him into the Wastelands if it's that important to you." Her eyes gleamed with challenge.

Fuck this. Morpheus wasn't going into the fucking Wastelands to follow the whelp. He was as good as dead out there, anyway. They hadn't brought any supplies with them and wouldn't last more than a day without shelter and water.

However, then Jeffos wouldn't have the whelp's head.

Rather than answer, Morpheus snarled and leapt forward, running at the Alpha bitch and the others. They spread out in a line at the mouth of the street—when Morpheus and his Alphas hit that line, he realized his mistake.

JORDAN

Breathing was agony. He could hear the sounds behind him. Hear the clash of battle. Hear the screams and the growls.

He kept moving forward. Kept running.

Well, as much as his current gait could be called running. It was a limping jog that became harder and harder to maintain with every step.

There were others around him. Cora's people. Guarding him. Escorting him.

All he had was the promise from Cora and Malachi that he wasn't about to be abandoned in the Wastelands. He didn't think this was a cruel trick. They might be ruthless, but they had their own honor. Unlike his father.

The door in the gate ahead loomed larger and larger as he ran toward the edges of civilization.

Did the sun already feel hotter? The air dryer and harder to breathe? Or did he feel this way because of his half-healed injuries?

Grimly, he went on. Knowing that he could do nothing for those behind him. Knowing he was headed to a part of the world most would consider certain death. Wondering if he was making the right choice.

ZADIA

Foolish, arrogant, and overconfident... all to Zadia's benefit. She almost laughed at the expression on Morpheus' face when he realized his mistake.

His forces were bottlenecked here. The street he'd led his forces down was more of a large alley, which meant her smaller team couldn't be surrounded by his overwhelming numbers. That didn't mean they couldn't be exhausted or that the line they'd formed wouldn't eventually be broken or forced back to where some could get by them, but it would give them time. So much precious time until Cora and the others could arrive.

She hoped Cora was bringing a lot of reinforcements. From what she could see, there were far too many Warguard... rows and rows of them going all the way back down the street.

Whether any of them would take initiative to go back down the alley and take a different route up the street... but Jeffos didn't have a reputation for rewarding initiative. She had to hope they'd wait, unmoving because Morpheus hadn't given them a direct order to go around.

He couldn't because he was too busy trying to kill Zadia, and for all his unthinking arrogance, he was a damn good fighter.

The only time Zadia had ever felt this overwhelmed was when she was sparring with Malachi. He moved in a blur, and she met each of his strikes but barely. Thankfully, he had gone right for her rather than Marcus or Vin, who were on either side of her. The Betas were battling for their lives, but neither of them would have been able to go toe to toe with Morpheus. She could barely stay on the defensive. If she managed to get a strike in, it would be a freaking miracle.

The knowledge she was likely facing her own death washed over her. She was not going to be able to match Morpheus forever. The best she could do was hold him off.

Pain slashed through her when she didn't dodge one of his blows quickly enough, leaving a slash across her unprotected hip. She growled, throwing her arms up to block another strike coming from above. Another slice of pain as one of his claws managed to get inside the joint of the armor on her arm.

Morpheus' eyes gleamed with triumph. He was going to win the fight, and they both knew it.

Trace

The sounds of battle grew louder in the dusty streets, the coppery smell of blood thickening the air. Trace's lips peeled back to show his teeth as he raced forward, running for the thick of it.

Movement at the opening of one of the streets, a line of fighters... and then one of them fell.

Zadia.

Her fall broke the line, and Alphas poured through, howling their triumph.

Snarling, Trace bounded forward even faster. Zadia wasn't one of his and Cora's, but he liked her. She reminded him of Cora. As she went down, so did the two males on either side of her, unable to hold their own as Morpheus passed them.

Trace's war cry rent the air. The snarls of the other Alphas beside him, those who had been keeping up with him, attracted the attention of Morpheus and the others. The Captain of the Warguard made a mocking motion of salute before shouting something at his soldiers.

The Warguard ran at Trace and the others—all of them except Morpheus, who took off in the other direction... following Jordan.

Fuck!

Trace threw himself into the thick of Alphas, tearing out the throat of the first one he reached. He waded through them as if they were a violent river, determined to get to the other side, determined to end Morpheus once and for all.

14

BLOOD & HEAT

Morpheus

Fuck.

Morpheus recognized the huge Alpha coming for him—Cora's co-Alpha, Trace. Skin dark as night, eyes colder than ice, he was rarely seen away from Cora's side, and Morpheus had never seen him fight. Until today, he would have assumed the Alpha's build was all for show. After all, what kind of Alpha male allowed a female to lead him around by the dick?

This was the first time Morpheus had seen Trace in action and realized he had vastly underestimated Cora's co-Alpha. Whatever his reason for letting Cora take the lead in their territory, it had nothing to do with his prowess as a fighter. Trace was cutting through the Warguard like a scythe through wheat, leaving blood and screams in his wake, heading for him with teeth bared and hate in his eyes.

Whether that emotion came from Morpheus and the Warguard's intrusion into Riversong territory, he couldn't possibly know, but he knew he had to defend himself. Frustration surged through him. None of this was going to plan. It should have been so much easier, yet here he was, in a fight for his life, while Jeffos sat back, safe and waiting for others to do his fighting for him.

The moment Trace reached him, Morpheus lashed out, aiming to land the first blow, draw the first blood. With almost supernatural speed, Trace brought his hand up, swiping Morpheus' hand away. The last time Morpheus had faced someone so fast, it had been the green-eyed Alpha who had saved Jeffos' son. Not a memory, nor a situation, he wanted to revisit.

He might have tried to talk to Trace, as he had to the Alpha bitch, but the male was intent on killing him. Morpheus had no breath to waste as he defended himself against Trace's furious blows. Claws swiped along his arm and shoulder, finding the spaces between his armor. Pain fought with adrenaline, and he ignored both.

A swipe across his face unleashed a furious growl, his chest rumbling threateningly, but it made no difference to Trace, who lashed out again. Snarling, Morpheus surged forward, the two Alphas clashing in a furious display of lethal aggression.

Trace was wearing less armor, yet no matter how many blows and swipes of his claw Morpheus landed, Trace didn't falter. He was relentless, and fear rose in Morpheus' breast.

I'm not even supposed to be here! I'm supposed to be collecting Jordan's head!

And the whelp was getting away.

Rather than lashing out with fists or kicks again, Morpheus lurched forward with his shoulder and shoved Trace into several of the other Warguard, who jumped him, trying to overwhelm him with their greater numbers. Breathing heavily, Morpheus backed away.

It was a strategic retreat.

Warring with Riversong's leaders was not the goal. Getting the whelp's head was. Once he had that, he could leave and return to Jeffos.

Turning, Morpheus moved through his own forces as they surged forward.

"No surrender!" he shouted, throwing his arm forward, pointing at Trace and the soldiers clashing with Riversong's additional forces. If Trace was here, he had no doubt Cora and more soldiers were close. He needed to get Jordan's head before this erupted into all-out war... if it wasn't already too late.

<u>MALACHI</u>

Hot, slick flesh parted for him as the heady scent of Tatiana's heat swirled in the air around them. Her nest was destroyed from their exertions, rumpled beyond repair and covered with their fluids. Yet Tatiana begged for more.

Hands pressing down on her wrists, he watched her arch beneath him, her slim legs pulling against his body, heels digging into his lower back as she pushed up against his steady thrusts. Every pulse of her body pulled at him, milking his seed from him with her muscles.

He wasn't sure she couldn't.

Each heat cycle was harder, more demanding, and he knew it was because every time, she took preventative measures when it was over, ensuring none of his seed took. They weren't ready for that yet.

But that didn't stop their bodies' demands. The craving. The driving need.

Grunting, Malachi moved harder, faster, his knot pushing inside her and expanding, pressing against the confines of her body even as her muscles pummeled the thick root. Ecstasy unraveled, washing over them as he spurted long ropes of fluid into her body, filling her yet again, while Tatiana keened in blissful satisfaction.

Half-collapsing on top of her, Malachi managed not to crush her. Not that he was sure she would care right now. Her muscles were still squeezing and milking his knot, squeezing every last ounce of pleasure and fluid from his body. Spent, she went limp beneath him, but he knew it wouldn't be long before she was reaching for him again.

It was up to him to stay sane, to keep them alive. An Omega in heat might forget to eat and drink as their instincts drove them. By the end, the Alpha with them could be just as drained.

This whole interlude was a massive risk.

He was trusting Cora and Trace not to betray him while he spent hours tending to Tatiana's needs.

He was trusting Zadia to keep Jeffos' son safe.

Trusting Jordan to be what he seemed.

Not being able to oversee everything himself was frustrating and worrying, but Tatiana's heat came first. That was the point of taking over from Jeffos. If he let her suffer without him, or if he let another Alpha take care of her needs when he knew she only wanted him, he wasn't any better than Jeffos. That was also why Jeffos would fail. He had no one he could trust. No one to allow him a few days' reprieve. Malachi did. So he used it.

And hoped nothing went wrong.

Jordan

Stumbling through the door, out of the Riversong territory and into the Wastelands, a feeling of victory swelled in Jordan's breast.

I made it.

He could barely breathe with the pain, the heat was already giving him a headache, and every one of his wounds ached, but he'd made it. The doors swung shut behind him with a clang. Relief and fear swirled in equal measure.

Relief because he knew some of the Warguard would be following him by now, and the doors would slow them down. Riversong's guards would stall them.

Fear because he was in the Wastelands and on his own.

Well. Mostly. He reached into his shirt, where a strap was hidden beneath the cloth, for the map. He needed to get to the rendezvous point and wait for Zadia and her team to meet him. He needed to get a move on because, eventually, those doors behind him would open. He had no idea how hard the soldiers would work to keep the Warguard from going through, and he wanted to be out of sight by then.

Glancing at the map, he tucked it back into his shirt next to the bladder, which held the bit of water he would have until he met up with Zadia and the others. His mouth was already parched from the heat, but he'd had plenty to drink before leaving this morning in anticipation of going into the Wastelands. He needed to wait until the need became much stronger before he indulged, or it would never last him. Since he'd needed to appear as though he was fleeing, it was a small container.

If this was nothing more than a ploy than to send him into the desert and die, at least he wouldn't suffer for too long, waiting for his inevitable end.

The stitch in his side easing, Jordan moved again, as fast as he could without hurting himself more, to meet the horizon.

CORA

Bodies lay in the street, hers and the Warguard's, and Cora snarled with rage at the sight. At least she could see Trace was still standing. Even among the crowd of Alphas, he stood out.

The forces she'd gathered slammed into the Warguard, joining the fight. To her surprise, once she got to Trace, shoving her way through the crowd, he shook his head, gesturing her on.

"Morpheus went to the gate!" Trace shouted over the din, deflecting another Alpha's strike before dealing him a lethal swipe of claws across his neck. Blood spurted, covering the side of Trace's face. He'd hit the jugular. With a gurgle, the Warguard Alpha went down, hand to his throat as if he thought he could stop the flow of his life force. Then he was just another body in the street, being trampled by those around him.

Fucking Jeffos.

He was happy to throw away the lives of his people while he stayed back, well out of danger. She couldn't wait to take him down. Make him pay for all of this.

The number of Warguard was still overwhelming, but she and Trace led her soldiers, breaking through the line on the other side, where the Warguard had nearly created a circle around them, and ran for the gate. She could see Morpheus and the others gathered around it in the distance.

So far, it remained closed.

Glancing over her shoulder, she was surprised and relieved to see the Warguard wasn't chasing her. All of her soldiers who had followed her and some of Trace's had made it through. Her chest twinged as she realized she didn't see Zadia, Vin, or Marcus among those running with them.

Damn.

They weren't hers, but she knew Malachi would feel their loss, and she'd liked Zadia. She saw a younger version of herself in the Alpha female.

Hearing them coming, Morpheus turned... and fled. His Warguard trailed behind him when they realized their leader was in full retreat, running down a side street that would lead him into no man's land, then back into Jeffos' territory.

The bastard.

Hell, no.

"Get him!" Cora screamed as rage pumped through her, making her run faster. Still fresh, since she hadn't been fighting like Trace, she pulled ahead of him, determined to reach Morpheus and make him pay. She couldn't get to Jeffos—yet—but Morpheus would be a worthy consolation prize.

15

RESCUE OR DEATH?

<u>Morpheus</u>

Running like his life depended on it—because it did—Morpheus panted for breath. Though it pained his pride to admit it, he knew he didn't have it in him to face Cora. Trace had nearly done him in, and Cora was fresh with energy. Now, his only goal was to return to Jeffos' territory.

The whelp had walked through the doors into the Wastelands—he'd seen it with his own eyes—and that would have to be good enough for Jeffos.

If the Warlord wanted his son's head, he should have come out and gotten it himself instead of sending Morpheus to do his dirty work. Jeffos always sent Morpheus while he sat back, issuing orders and expecting his will to be done. Enough was enough. Morpheus was not giving up his life so Jeffos could have a trophy he would never have won himself.

Crossing from Riversong territory into no man's land, Morpheus' steps didn't slow. The pounding footsteps of the guard around and beside him didn't either. None of them wanted to take on Cora's soldiers. The Warguard might have outnumbered them, but

Morpheus had split his people, and Cora's followers were fresh and frothing at the mouth for a chance to fight.

Morpheus just wanted to get back home.

A cry sounded, then suddenly cut off behind him, letting him know that at least one of his males had fallen. He didn't glance over his shoulder. Nothing would slow him down.

His lungs felt as if they were about to burst as he pelted through the abandoned streets, not knowing how many of his Alphas were still with him. How many had made it out alive? How many were back with the first group, battling Trace and the others. Morpheus had no doubt Cora's forces were the only ones chasing him. They would not have left other Warguard in their territory unchecked.

The streets of Jeffos' territory loomed ahead, and Morpheus would have crowed with glee if he'd had the breath. Running faster, harder, he put his head down and sprinted for safety.

<u>Cora</u>

Fuck.

Cora slowed her steps.

Morpheus and about ten of his guard had outrun her. Her soldiers slowed with her, and they stood at the edge of no man's land, glaring into Jeffos' territory. Her instincts told her to follow—the retreat was a show of weakness that stirred her desire to kill—but she would be in enemy territory and wasn't ready for that. She didn't know where the rest of the Warguard was and would not waste her people on a useless foray into another's streets. Unlike Jeffos. The fucker.

Although she wanted to.

Unfortunately, even ending Morpheus wouldn't end all this. There were still more Warguard. More Alphas. Jeffos himself.

But it was a nice thought.

Whirling around, she gestured to her soldiers. Staring after

Morpheus and wishing she'd caught up to him was a waste of precious time.

"Back to Trace and the others," she barked out. The five who had followed her through the melee did an about-face, opening enough space to let her through, so they could follow her once more.

Doing nothing but running was driving her crazy.

She wanted to kill something.

TRACE

The Warguard had retreated, and the walls of the streets that had hemmed them in now helped them. Trace snarled, pressing forward, ignoring the blood seeping from his many wounds and the pain that wove its way through his body, weakening him.

If nothing else, he would buy Cora time. Keep her from ending up between Morpheus' forces and these as best he could. If he fell, he fell. They were already walking on bodies, slipping and sliding over broken limbs and skulls, trying to continue the fight. Another one would hardly go noticed, even if it was his.

Breaking into a full retreat, the Warguard turned and ran... and Trace let them. Panting for breath, he fell to his knees, watching them go. Around him, so did the others.

Despite being massively outnumbered, somehow, they'd ended up victorious... as long as Jordan had made it into the Wastelands. Trace closed his eyes. He'd better have, or this was all for naught.

"Trace!" Cora's voice broke through.

He turned his head and opened his eyes. His dark beauty came running down the same street she'd gone up, retracing her path, which would have avoided the fleeing Warguard, and he was glad for it. He could see the fire in her eyes, anger at having been denied her own battle.

He'd never seen such a beautiful sight.

"Cora." His voice was hoarse, the insides of his throat ravaged from snarling and bellowing out what directions he'd been able to. A moment later, she was there, wrapping her arms protectively around his shoulders and pulling his head into her stomach.

Safe.

It was the first time he'd felt the need to shelter against Cora, but he'd never battled such an overwhelming force of Warguard.

"The fuckers ran." Her voice vibrated with fury at their perimeter having been breached. "We'll need to double our guards." What she didn't say was they would also need to double their silent watchers. If it wasn't for Grigori...

Trace hated being indebted to that two-faced weasel, but credit where credit was due. Their plans would have come to naught if it wasn't for him. If they hadn't already.

"Jordan got out?"

"Yes." Clawed fingertips swept over his head, gently probing for bumps and bruises.

His head was mostly unscathed, though there were a few scrapes and scratches. His left arm had taken the most damage. At least part of their plan had gone correctly.

"Alpha! Zadia is missing!"

Trace stiffened as Cora's fingers stilled, his eyes popping open to stare at the soldier who stood at the mouth of the street, surrounded by bodies.

"She fell," he grated out. Not only fallen, but she'd fallen right where the majority of the fight had taken place—her body would have been trampled even if she hadn't been dead when she'd gone down.

"Is anyone else missing?" Cora's question came out as a short, sharp demand.

Forcing himself to his feet, Trace joined in the painful process of combing through the dead, looking for their own.

By the time they had finished, they knew Zadia's was the only body missing. Because she'd been leading the way? Because she had somehow, miraculously, survived? Or for some other unknown and likely unpalatable reason?

They had no way of knowing.

Gathering their dead, they left the bodies of the Warguard burning in a heap, with a few left to watch, so the fire didn't spread. Of Morpheus and the rest of the Warguard, there was no further sign.

TATIANA

Need.

Her throat was parched. Muscles ached. Both seemed minor compared to the need pulsing through her.

More, more, more.

She crawled her way up Malachi's hard body, hands and mouth exploring, lapping at the fluids coating his thighs and groin. He groaned in his sleep, hands moving restlessly to find her tangled hair.

The rigid length of his erection grew under her lips until pearly nectar leaked from the tip. Tatiana eagerly fell upon it, lapping it with her tongue. Her lips engulfed the tip, then moved downward, coaxing more from his body, drinking it down.

It quenched the thirst, though it did nothing for the need pulsing between her thighs.

Malachi rumbled, a low Alpha's growl that flowed through the air and sank into her bones. His hand tightened in her hair. The fluid leaking from his tip became a small stream as she suckled. Tatiana's insides clenched and pulsed, sending a small gush of slick from her body.

Releasing him from her mouth, she climbed atop him. Weary muscles did not matter. Straddling his hips, she pressed his thick sword against her opening and sank onto it. Flesh parted, filling her, completing her, and her head fell back in a whimpering moan.

One hand still in her hair, the other moved up her body to close around her breast, squeezing painfully and plucking at the sensitive nipple. The tiny bud plumped in response, begging for more.

Hands on his chest, Tatiana rose and fell, her thighs pushing up and relaxing, her inner muscles clenching and quivering around his thickness as she impaled herself over and over. Slick gushed from her, coating his cock and groin, making it easier for her to use him as her body demanded.

Still, it wasn't enough.

"Please... Malachi... please..." She squirmed atop him, needing more, needing his dominance.

A low chuckle. Another pinch to her nipple.

She was flipped onto her back with a suddenness that took her breath away. Who needed air, anyway? She didn't. Not nearly as badly as she needed him inside her, pounding away between her thighs, the delicious friction sending her closer and closer to writhing ecstasy.

The thick knot shoved into her again, pressing against her glands, sending shockwaves of pleasure rippling through her. She arched, thrusting her hips up to meet him, crying out and clawing at his chest as he forced his knot into her again. The thick bulge expanded, locking them together as she shrieked with satisfied ecstasy, her body pulling, milking, wanting more of him, as much as she could take. His seed flooded her, the knot keeping any from leaking out of her as much as it locked them together.

"Malachi!"

JORDAN

Sitting in the meager shade offered by the outcropping, he was fairly certain was the meeting point, Jordan was beginning to worry. He'd known Zadia and the others would be behind him, but they should have been here by now. Since he'd been so focused on getting into the Wastelands, he hadn't been able to take the time to really look at the number of Warguard who had attacked, but he was worried it was enough that they'd won.

Was anyone coming? Or was he going to die out here in the Wastelands, not because of intention, but because their plan had been thwarted?

His water was already half gone, and he was panting from the heat, despite the shade. While he still sweated a bit, it wasn't as much as he should. If help didn't arrive before nightfall, it wouldn't matter since he would freeze without any kind of protection.

Looking back in the direction he'd come from, he blinked when he saw dust rising from the land.

Grabbing hold of the rock, he got to his feet.

There was no wind to stir the earth. That was the mark of someone in the distance, coming closer.

Hope and wariness rose in equal measure, and he squinted, trying to see better. Friend or foe?

Rescue or an earlier death than expected?

16

EXECUTION

Jordan

The small group came closer, dust stirring beneath their feet from the dry land as they moved. Unsure whether they were Malachi's people or his father's, Jordan refused to sit down, no matter how much effort it took him to remain on his feet. If they were Warguard, he would be dead in a few minutes and refused to die sitting down.

At the front was a large Alpha with tanned skin and dark hair. It took a moment for Jordan to recognize him as one of the males he'd seen at the Wolf's headquarters, another of the Wolf's lieutenants... but not Zadia.

"You look like you're about to fall over," Marek said, his dark eyes sharp. Jordan scowled but knew Marek wasn't wrong. Still, admitting to any hint of weakness went against his instincts. "Sit down. Finish whatever water you have. We have more. We need to get the shelters up. There's a storm coming."

The words jerked everyone into movement. Jordan uncapped his water and chugged it down, watching as the males with Marek got to work. Marek climbed up onto the outcropping of rocks, looking off into the distance.

"How long?" Jordan asked. Storms in the Wastelands could come in many forms. Acidic rain that burned and sizzled on the skin. Sand that stripped flesh from bone. Hail the size of small boulders. Unknown elements that left no trace behind.

The shelters Cora had sent with them would withstand one, maybe two, storms at the most. They were costly to make, heavy to carry, and so ineffective after one or two uses, they were extremely rare and only used in the direst of circumstances because they were so unreliable.

She'd offered them up without hesitation, though, in service to the plan.

"Less than an hour." Marek's lips curved as he jumped down. "Any of the Warguard caught out on this side of the wall won't make it home tonight." The big Alpha cast a critical eye over the shelters the betas with him had erected.

"Done, Alpha," one of them said with a respectful nod.

The betas under the Wolf, Cora, and Trace, weren't expected to bow and scrape the way they were for Jeffos, but they did show respect to the Alphas. Jorden found it odd, but he liked it better than the fearful cowering of Jeffos' betas. He had to admit, he had not thought much about their plight before.

"Jordan, you'll be with me and Bran." He motioned to Jordan.

The shelters were like tents but had steel under their fabric and not much give. It would be cramped quarters with another Alpha, but he didn't blame Marek. While Jordan was still weak and the betas were good fighters, there was no reason to take chances on the Warlord's son.

He didn't protest as he got into the shelter with Marek.

Morpheus

The return to the Warlord's stronghold was one of trepidation. Morpheus straggled in, the rank smell of fear permeating the air around him. Not only his, but all of his soldiers who had made it back with him.

They knew the Warlord did not look kindly upon failure, and Morpheus had never had to report so complete a defeat to him before. Then they had not gone up against Cora and Trace for a reason. Morpheus gritted his teeth against his anger at Jeffos for sending them out without preparation or forethought.

It would do no good.

Maybe he should have pushed back harder, but when it came to his son, Jeffos was apparently deaf to reason.

Perhaps...

Perhaps this was Morpheus' chance. The Warlord had always been canny, unbeatable... but this was a weakness he hadn't realized before. One he could use if he was careful.

Looking around at the demoralized state of his warriors, he didn't think any of them would be against ending Jeffos' reign.

Until then, he still had to face the Warlord.

Glancing around, he grimaced as he only counted ten males still with him.

How had he managed to lose forty? The loss was staggering. Debilitating. They would have to push forward the next crop of Alphas to being designated Warguard immediately, even if they were a little younger and less trained than Morpheus would like. Their youth didn't count against them, exactly, but the stupidity and immaturity they displayed because of their age did. Still, as cannon fodder went, there were worse options. They would be vicious in their need to prove themselves, which was exactly what Morpheus needed right now.

"Come with me," he ordered the ten soldiers still with him. The expressions on their faces were wary, but they obeyed, following him as he made the grim walk to Jeffos' throne room. In his head, he tried to think of what he could say to placate the Warlord.

The door to the room was slightly ajar, and Morpheus could hear voices inside. Frowning, he picked up his pace and heard his Warguard do the same behind him.

When he pushed the door fully open, he was relieved to see there were more of his Warguard inside. They must have escaped separately and made their way back. Thank the stars, he hadn't actually lost forty of them.

Their presence also meant that Jeffos already knew the bad news.

Morpheus mentally braced himself for the Warlord's rage, but if it was present, it wasn't evident when Morpheus looked up at Jeffos' face. The Alpha's expression was tight, not red or full of fury, the way Morpheus had imagined it would be. Maybe he was finally seeing reason.

"There you are." The unfamiliar voice came from the pack of Warguard, and Morpheus jerked his head around. Chadrick stepped out from the pack, his head lifted, a sneer on his lips. "I shouldn't have doubted your survival instincts. You saved yourself and left the rest of us to die."

"I did what any good commander would and focused on the mission," Morpheus corrected, rage welling up inside of him. The arrogant Alpha was due a reminder of who was the Captain of the Warguard.

"And? How did the mission go?" Jeffos interrupted icily. "I don't see my son."

Straightening, Morpheus stood at attention as he faced Jeffos head-on. He knew the Warlord would not be happy with the lack of Jordan's head, but he was going to have to accept the reality of the situation.

"He was chased into the Wastelands by Cora's people. There's nothing for him out there but death."

"I wanted his *head*," Jeffos seethed, gripping the arms of his chair. Now the unhinged fury reared its head, holding the Warlord firmly in its grasp. The Alpha's chest heaved, his eyes blazed, and the steel throne beneath him creaked as his muscles flexed. It was as though the entire room took a deep breath in and held it, waiting to see what he would do. "You should have followed him. Caught up with him. 'As good as dead' is not 'dead.'"

"We would have had to fight our way through Riversong's wall gate or returned to our own, then gone out. We were not prepared for such an excursion. There would have been nothing but death for all of us."

The logic of his words didn't seem to matter to Jeffos, who growled, getting to his feet. It took all of Morpheus' willpower not to step back. Jeffos' mere presence could be overwhelming, not just his size but the power and confidence with which he held himself, and when that was all focused on one person, it could be terrifying. However, Morpheus was a powerful Alpha, too. He lifted his chin, even as others bowed their heads.

He was Captain of the Warguard and would face his leader's wrath with his head held high.

"So, instead, you chose defeat and dishonor?" The Warlord's tone was low. Lethal. The steel in Morpheus' spine trembled.

"There is no dishonor in a tactical retreat, especially when we were already being defeated." Though he doubted the Warlord had ever had to retreat in his life, but then he wasn't the one out on the front line, was he? He had sent Morpheus in his place. Morpheus would like to see the Warlord go head-to-head with Trace, but no, Jeffos sat back and let others do his work for him. "You would have made the same choice."

"Never." Jeffos' eyes blazed. "You are a coward and are hereby relieved of your command."

"You're demoting me? Who the hell do you think can run the Warguard without me?"

"Me." Chadrick stepped forward from behind Jeffos, grinning smugly. Morpheus growled. "I gathered up the soldiers you abandoned, took a prisoner, and led us back to the Stronghold."

"You—" Morpheus didn't get the words out before Jeffos sprang forward.

For all of Morpheus' doubts about Jeffos' current abilities, they were wiped away. He was faster than Trace, stronger, too, and Morpheus had no chance of dodging the hand that wrapped around his throat. He swung his arm, trying to hammer down on Jeffos' inner elbow to force the Warlord to release him, but it was like hitting a brick wall.

The only other time Morpheus had faced something like this was when the green-eyed Alpha had intervened with Jordan's execution. Except he'd been taken off guard, too convinced Jeffos needed him. He hadn't seen the danger until it was too late.

Flesh tore, a wet gurgle filling his ears, and warmth flowed over his chest before he collapsed into a heap on the floor.

Jeffos

Licking the blood from his fingertips, Jeffos turned to face Chadrick. The young Alpha preened.

"Get someone to clean this up," Jeffos said, gesturing to the bloody heap of his former Captain of the Warguard. Morpheus had outlived his usefulness. Jeffos had seen the flash of rebellion in his once-loyal captain's eyes.

He had no use for someone who could not follow directions.

As he stalked out of the room, he heard Chadrick ordering the others about removing the body. How long he would be able to hold on to his new title remained to be seen, but for now, he was making himself useful. He was too stupid to realize his best asset was he was young and moldable, though he had also been quick enough to take captive the female Alpha leading the squad chasing Jordan.

She was sure to be full of vital information.

And breaking her would be a pleasure.

17

UNCERTAINTY & REWARDS

Cora

"How much longer, do you think?" Cora asked. Trace glanced at her, lifting his eyebrow as if questioning what she was speaking about. There were two choices.

Marek's return with Jordan or the end of Tatiana's heat.

The former had been gone for a full day, and soldiers on the wall had reported seeing signs of a storm passing over in the direction of where they were supposed to rendezvous. Even with the shelters Cora had provided, there was always a chance none of them would return.

"For Marek and Jordan," she clarified. "I would be surprised if Malachi and Tatiana finish today. Perhaps tomorrow."

The run of an Omega's heat could be unpredictable, but it usually lasted at least forty-eight full hours. Cora wouldn't plan on any sooner, for certain. Trace nodded thoughtfully, his thoughts easily following hers, the way they often did.

"Hopefully, soon." Trace's gaze moved back out the window, past the gates at the end of the courtyard below, as if willing them to appear.

The answer was frustrating because it was exactly what she

already knew, yet she'd felt compelled to ask anyway. Sitting around doing nothing, waiting, when there were so many events out of her control—she could be very patient, but there were times when she didn't like it very much.

Usually, she could find something to do, but right now, her hands were tied as she waited for others to finish what they were doing. There was something niggling at the back of her mind, though... something forgotten. Something important.

Pressing her lips together, she slowly tapped her nails against the wooden table beneath her fingertips, trying to remember what it was. Trace turned to look at her again, a question in his eyes, as her fingers stilled.

"Trace," she said slowly. "Where is Grigori?"

GRIGORI

"Jeffos has executed his captain and promoted another alpha in his place. Twenty-five of the Warguard were killed, and seven of Cora's betas and one of her alphas was taken captive."

"Interesting." The voice on the other end of the receiver said after a thoughtful moment. "But not enough."

Fury seethed through Grigori.

"War will break out any day. These are just the initial skirmishes. You cannot promise my safety if there is fighting, in which case, you are not useful to me. So far, all you have done is make empty promises."

It was a risk, challenging his ally, but one he was willing to take because time was running out. He could feel it slipping through his fingers. While Zone One might not be taking his information seriously, Grigori could smell the winds of change in the air. He needed to get himself and Tatiana out of the territories before that happened, or all of his hard work was for naught.

There was another long pause, and Grigori was about to drop the comm unit in disgust when the voice finally answered.

"You are correct that we have requested much while not rewarding you. The next chance you get, go to the wall. Box 74263, passcode 78632339. A reward for the work you've done so far is inside. Got that?"

Thankfully, Grigori had always had an easy time with numbers. He would need to repeat it several times to himself as he made his way there, but he would remember.

"74263, passcode 78632339."

"Good. Contact me again when they're going to do more than skirmish."

The line went dead, and Grigori sneered. Skirmish? Ha. That had been the opening gambit of the war, and his contact knew it. He was downplaying it so he could leave Grigori's accomplishments unacknowledged. One day, once he was part of Zone One, he would work until his contact was his inferior, reporting to him, and he was going to love every second.

Hiding the comm unit back in its place, he made his way along the rooftops to the wall boxes, avoiding Cora's sentries. They were good. They didn't neglect to have checkpoints along the tops of buildings, and the sentries in the street often looked up, but he was better. It didn't hurt that he had looked at the routes and schedule while nosing around her headquarters.

The wall boxes were where the few items that were traded between Zone One and the territories were passed through. Very few knew their passcodes, and they were changed with regularity, though the boxes themselves were used rarely.

Grigori was not surprised to find no one near them in the territories. On the Zone's wall, however, he saw someone looking over the edge, noting his presence, then turning to walk away. Probably to report in that Grigori had actually arrived.

That was fine with him. He deserved a reward for everything he'd been through, working for the Zone with no kind of recompense so far.

Quickly finding the right box, he punched in the code and waited for a moment. It was one of the smaller boxes since the goods passed through were often in large shipments when they went, but the parcel inside was even smaller. Stepping in, Grigori scooped it from the ground and hurried away with it. The box's steel door ominously shut behind him on its own as he retreated to the streets of the surrounding territory.

He didn't stop to open the small parcel until he was well away from the Zone, as if someone there might try to snatch it back from him if he lingered too long. Not that he was sure whatever was in the parcel would be worth all this.

Unwrapping the paper, he breathed out a low breath as the small bottle, packed with little white powder-filled capsules, came into view. There were so many jammed in, it didn't make any noise when he shook it gently.

There was no mistaking the markings on the capsules, though—these were the suppressors that would inhibit Tatiana's omega nature.

Too late for this heat, but it would have other benefits. He could slip this into her food, and once her Omega need for Malachi was gone, that would be Grigori's chance to show her everything she could have living as a beta... with him.

JORDAN

Laying in place for hours, the wind screaming above them as heat and sand scoured the shelters, the noise far too loud to allow for conversation, was not something Jordan had ever thought he'd have to do. The air grew musty and hot enough to make his lungs hurt when he breathed in and his body temperature far too warm.

Whatever was in the storm above them, it must be at least a thousand degrees for them to feel it within the tents.

When it was finally over, he was exhausted. Every muscle in his body had been tense the entire time. Neither he, Marek, nor the beta with them had managed any sleep. Emerging, there was no relief. The Wastelands were as dry and hot as ever. Jordan felt parched from the inside out.

One of the betas inspected what looked like char marks on the outcropping beside them before muttering something under his breath. The others were looking over the tents.

"These won't last through another storm," one of them said. Tugging gently at the fabric on the outside, it peeled away easily.

"Then we need to get moving." Marek's statement was obvious, yet saying it out loud made everything feel more ominous. "We need to make it back inside the walls. Keep an eye out for Warguard."

They weren't returning to the same exit from Riversong they'd gone through, instead heading toward one farther away from No Man's Land and Jeffos' territory. Farther from where they were now.

Jordan kept pace with the others, but it hurt. He could feel his injuries tugging at him, blood slowly rising to the surface and sluggishly seeping through his clothing where one of them had reopened. When he began to drop back behind the others, he stayed silent, kept his head down, and kept moving.

He would not ask them to slow, risking their own lives for him again. Not after hearing the storm and knowing there were no more adequate shelters to be had. The wall between the Wastelands and the territories loomed ahead as they approached, but they were nowhere near the door yet.

Marek shifted direction, so they were angling along the wall's perimeter rather than heading straight toward it. Which was when he looked back over his shoulder at Jordan. Holding up his hand, he slowed the others and ran back. Jordan had dropped even farther back by then.

"Fool, why didn't you say anything?" Marek wrapped his arm around Jordan's back, looping Jordan's arm over his shoulders to help support him as they kept moving.

Fuck, that hurt. Jordan grit his teeth against the pain, breathing through it before he could answer, his voice tight.

"I'll still make it, just a bit behind you all."

"You'll make it with us. I will not fail this mission."

"This mission isn't worth your life." *I'm not worth your life.*

Already, far too many had died helping Jordan escape from the city. Even knowing it had been part of the plan, he knew they hadn't expected the number of Warguard Jeffos had sent to retrieve him.

"This mission? No. What this mission will get us when we return with you and can begin hounding Jeffos? Yes." The utter conviction in Marek's voice made Jordan hold his tongue.

The other Alpha was dedicated to his cause, and he would not be swayed.

An hour later, Marek on one side and a beta on the other, Jordan finally returned to Riversong.

18

TELL ME EVERYTHING

Tatiana

When she woke, Tatiana knew her heat was over and sighed in relief before rolling onto her back and groaning. Her whole body ached, inside and out, and she felt as if she'd run a marathon.

"Shhh. Drink." Malachi's deep voice was soft, gentle. The way it always was at the end of her heat.

He helped her sit up, pressing a cup to her lips for her to drink long, slow sips of water. Though she'd drunk plenty of his thick seed during her heat, she hadn't had much water. The sexual need always overrode everything else.

As the cool water flowed down her throat into her mostly-empty stomach, Tatiana felt more herself. Rational thought was returning, along with the worry. Lifting her hands, she put them over Malachi's, greedily drinking more and more as her thirst and hunger could finally be felt.

"How long?" she asked when she finally pulled away.

"Two and a half days." There was no censure in his voice, but Tatiana still winced. Two and a half crucial days, when Malachi had to tend to her rather than advance the plans he'd made. Events had flown past them while they'd been inured in this room. The scent of sweat and musk hung heavy in the air, a stark reminder of what they'd spent that time doing, shut away from the world and its events.

She closed her eyes. "I'm sorry."

He should have sent someone else to her in his place, even though every part of her cringed at the idea. Her weakness, her Omega nature, was the problem.

"Never apologize for what you are." Malachi's fingertips touched beneath her chin, and she opened her eyes to look up at him. "You are an Omega. That is precious. It is something to be treasured."

Except it cost him. Tatiana bit her lip, but she didn't argue with him. She knew he would not change his mind. If she wasn't an Omega, she never would have been in danger, never needed saving, and would never have met him. The heat was what had brought him to her in the first place.

Now, it was a liability. Whether or not he was willing to admit it, she would not hide the truth from herself. Hopefully, it would not become too much of one.

"Did the plan work?" she asked hopefully. Malachi hesitated, and her guilt swelled.

"It is *not* your fault," he said sternly.

Pressing her lips together to keep from arguing, Tatiana nodded. He had that look on his face, the one that said he wasn't going to put up with any arguments from her, even if he was wrong.

While it might not be her fault she'd was born an Omega, it was her fault for not being able to withstand her nature. She should have pushed him harder to let her suffer through the heat on her own or send another Alpha to service her. Even now, she was selfish enough to be relieved he'd done neither and stayed with her. Guilt suffused her as much as relief.

"Jeffos sent a larger force than we anticipated, but Cora and Trace saw it through. Jordan escaped into the Wastelands and returned safely."

There was something he wasn't telling her. Otherwise, he wouldn't have hesitated at first.

"What else happened?" She rose onto her knees and poked her

finger in his chest. There was a somberness to him she was just now noticing.

"Zadia." Malachi said her name with a grimace, and Tatiana's heart leapt in her throat. "It's not as bad as it could be. Trace thought she'd been killed, but Grigori brought back word that she was taken captive."

A female Alpha in Jeffos' hands? Tatiana wasn't sure that was better than being dead. Though there was hope for rescue, she could only imagine what Zaida's treatment would be like in the meantime, and it didn't bear thinking about.

Grigori had brought back word? Putting himself in danger again to collect information. Fear rose in her, making her shake her head. He was so desperate to prove himself, he took unnecessary risks, yet she couldn't be too angry because otherwise, they might not have known about Zadia.

"Cora and Trace want to talk to me about mounting a rescue." Malachi's finger stroked down Tatiana's cheek as she released a breath, she hadn't realized she was holding.

There had been part of her that feared Malachi and the others would leave Zadia where she was. There were greater concerns than one soldier, but that wasn't how Malachi operated. He always took care of his own.

"Go then," Tatiana breathed. As much as she wanted him to remain with her, to cuddle and pretend the rest of the world didn't exist, she'd taken up too much of his time. Zadia was far more important than her desire to snuggle.

The purr that rumbled from his chest didn't help her desires, but it was nice. His lips claimed hers for a kiss.

"Grigori is waiting for you in the outer chamber," he said, just before he left. "Do you want to see him?"

Did she? She would have liked some time to herself, but Grigori would be able to catch her up on events and wouldn't try to shield her the way Malachi did. She was sure there was more Malachi was leaving out, not wanting to hurt her. Tatiana nodded.

"Tell him I will be there in a few minutes."

Malachi nodded, then was gone.

Groaning, Tatiana forced her tired muscles to move and quickly wiped herself down with water from the basin on the side of the room. Later, she would take a bath to help ease her aches and pains, but for now, this would have to do. She didn't want to keep Grigori waiting too long.

When she entered the outer chamber, she wished she had made him wait a little longer. His nose wrinkled the moment she walked in. She blushed, realizing the scent of her and Malachi's combined passion must be even stronger than she'd realized.

"Are you hungry?" Grigori asked, his face back to its neutral expression. He waved a hand at the table in the center of the room that was laden with food. "There's enough to feed an army."

Tatiana's mouth watered, and her stomach rumbled. She was ravenous, as she always was after a heat. In Malachi's presence, her stomach hadn't been her first concern, but now that he was gone, her body's demands were coming back full force.

"Yes." She sat down at the table, yanking a plate of meat toward her as she caught Grigori's eye. "Catch me up? Tell me everything."

Jordan

"Tell me everything."

The Alpha's demand wasn't unexpected. As far as Jordan knew, Malachi had only been briefly updated before he had to return to Tatiana. Now that her heat was definitely over, he clearly wished to be fully informed.

Jordan spoke first, then Trace, then Marek. Throughout, Malachi's expression remained impassive, but his green eyes were glinting with emotion, especially when Trace mentioned Zadia.

When Marek finished, Cora finally spoke up.

"Grigori says Zadia's injuries were numerous, but we all know Jeffos has healers at his disposal if he wishes her brought back to full health. So far, there's been no mention of an execution."

"We all know he would make it a spectacle to make her an example, if that's what he was going to do," Marek murmured. His jaw clenched, and Jordan realized his own was as well.

Even though it hadn't been his plan, even though he hadn't been part of that fight, he still felt partially responsible for Zadia's fate.

"He's had her for two days. If she was going to die from her injuries, we'd know about it by now." Cora dropped her gaze to the map on the center of the table. It was the one Jordan had helped draw, outlining every inch of the Warlord's dungeons, which were extensive.

"Has the new Captain of the Guard done anything?" Malachi asked.

Jordan had to shake his head with wonder. Part of him still didn't believe that Morpheus was dead. Perhaps part of him didn't want to believe—it made him feel cheated of his own revenge.

Cora snorted. "Other than parade through the streets and have his Alphas beat up a few betas? No. That can't last, though. He will need to prove himself, or he'll be quickly replaced."

"Taking a valuable captive will give him some leeway from my father, but not from the other Alphas." Jordan shook his head. Morpheus' death left open a power vacuum that was more than a little dangerous. He still couldn't believe his father's short-sightedness.

Perhaps his father wasn't as canny as Jordan had believed.

Or perhaps he was finally going mad from the power he'd amassed and the mistakes he'd made. Jordan could only hope. He also worried there was another unknown factor he was missing.

"We'll need to move fast," Cora murmured, her finger trailing along the corridor where Jordan had told them his father kept high-profile prisoners, the ones he actually wanted to keep alive for a while.

The accommodations there were a little better. The ones on the level beneath it were where prisoners were left to rot. They had no value, and once they went in, they never came out again. The cells were dank, freezing, and the only food and water was what could be scavenged from within the cells. As far as Jordan knew, most of those poor souls didn't last a week.

"Zadia knows everything about our plans for Jordan."

<u>ZADIA</u>

The healers didn't speak a word to her, which was how she knew she wasn't home, despite the fever dreams. Sometimes Malachi spoke to her. Sometimes Cora.

But they weren't really there.

"I need her healed! What is taking so long?" The words were right for Malachi, but the tone was wrong. There was no concern for her.

There was an answering murmur, not placating but fearful.

I am in enemy hands.

Don't forget. Don't forget. Don't forget.

This is not home.

She would rather have the fever take her than betray her people.

19

DECISIONS & CONFRONTATIONS

Grigori

Watching Tatiana stuff her face with food, Grigori hid his distaste. She looked gaunt, even though this heat had been a shorter one. Seeing the toll it took on her body always stirred his emotions.

This time, though, rather than seeming satisfied and unnaturally happy, she was morose.

"Did something happen between you and Malachi?" Grigori asked, forcing himself to leave the hope he felt out of his voice.

"What?" Tatiana blinked, focusing on him as if she'd forgotten he was there. She shook her head. "No, of course not... it's just..." She sighed, looking down at her food. Her voice was quieter when she spoke again. "This heat came at such a bad time. I can't believe everything that happened... and Malachi... he should have been there for it. If he was, Zadia might never have been captured." Tears filled her voice, which made Grigori want to shake his head, but then Tatiana had always been soft-hearted.

"It was not good timing," he agreed, taking some pleasure in her flinch. Was there ever good timing for a heat? He didn't think so. It was nice to see her finally acknowledging the downside of being an Omega, something she hadn't done since meeting Malachi. Finally, she might be ready to hear his offer again, and this time, he had the goods to back it up. "But you can change that."

Pressing her lips together, Tatiana lifted her head to meet his gaze again.

"You're talking about the suppressors again. It's a nice thought, at least until this all over, but who knows if you could even get any before my next heat." Her voice was flat, unhappy, but hope and happiness filled Grigori's chest. She wasn't turning down his suggestion out of hand. It sounded like she'd thought about the logistics.

"I have them now." He moved closer, sliding onto the seat next to her, enjoying the way her mouth dropped open in shock. "I have them, and you can start them now. You won't have to worry about your heat interfering again."

Once she realized how much better her life was without her Omega attributes, once she was free of the demands nature had put on her, she wouldn't have to worry about it interfering with anything *ever* again. She'd take the suppressors, they'd escape to Zone One as soon as his contact was satisfied, and he'd never have to deal with the territories or the damn Alphas ever again.

The day couldn't come too soon.

"You have them?" Disbelief and hope filled her voice as she turned to him, desperation in her dark eyes. She was still speaking in a whisper, as though afraid someone might overhear. "You actually have suppressors? How?"

"I have a source. Here." Grigori pulled the bottle from his pocket, handing them to her, ready to snatch them back if he needed to, but he didn't need to worry. Events had pressed her into a corner.

"How many?" she asked as she opened it. "How often?"

"One a day, every day." Triumph filled him as she popped the pill into her mouth and swallowed convulsively.

Finally.

JORDAN

"We're going to move up the plans with you." Malachi's eyes roved over the map of the dungeon. "You will be our distraction. We didn't know until now how obsessed your father is with you, but now that we do, I will use it."

Jordan nodded. Hiding away for several months hadn't been at the top of his list of things to do, but he would have done it. Disappearing for months. then reappearing would drive his father wild. That had never been in doubt.

Malachi was right; his father was far more focused on him than he would have predicted. It would be foolish not to use that obsession. Especially now that Jeffos had shown his hand.

"Will he still throw his forces away, though?" Cora murmured, finger tapping thoughtfully against her lip as though she was talking more to herself than to the rest of them. "Or will he have learned his lesson?"

"I want to at least try." Malachi cocked his head to the side. "If it doesn't work, we'll put him in hiding again. Doing so would still work to our advantage. The Warlord will be distracted by whether he's willing to continue throwing the Warguard after Jordan."

"He'll likely send some. If Morpheus was killed for failing to retrieve me, the new captain would feel compelled to capture me, even if Jeffos doesn't give the command."

"True." Cora smiled widely. Behind her, Trace nodded his head, though no smile showed on his face. He rarely smiled, as far as Jordan could tell. The Alpha was still injured from the battle a few days before, though recovering. He was in better shape than Jordan was, though Jordan was finally able to move more freely and without as much pain. "Between the two of them, the mere whisper of Jordan's presence will be like lighting a tinderbox."

"We'll start tomorrow," Malachi said decisively. His green eyes were cold as they met Jordan's, the power of his Alpha nature curling around him, unseen but felt by all. The only time Jordan had ever felt its like was when he was in the presence of his father, which was why he was convinced Malachi might be the person to finally unseat the Warlord. "We'll have you show yourself to a squadron of Warguard and see what happens. We will have to decide what to do from there, but we are not letting Zadia rot in the Warlord's prison for months."

What no one said aloud was it was very unlikely Zaida would be left to rot, regardless.

CHADRICK

Chadrick had more sympathy for Morpheus in death than he had in life. The old Captain of the Guard had commanded a certain amount of respect, even though he'd been surrounded by fellow Alphas, none of who truly wanted to follow another's orders.

They were all eying him as if they thought they could do a better job. In fact, he was pretty sure the only reason he hadn't been challenged yet was none of them were sure they *wanted* the job right now. The Warlord was far more demanding and unreasonable than Chadrick had realized.

Morpheus had always stood as a buffer between the Warlord and the Warguard, and now, Chadrick was the one standing in his place.

His balls ached as he stared straight ahead at the Warlord, doing his best to ignore the mewling Omega on the Alpha's lap. As the Warlord's ungentle hands were exploring her body, her eyes glazed with lust, and the scent of her arousal filled the room. There were other guards in the room, there always were, but Chadrick had underestimated how disturbing it was to be unable to look away from the display.

When he'd been a regular guard, he hadn't had to look the Warlord in the face as he played with his Omega. Hadn't had to try as hard to keep his eyes from the Omega's smooth curves and dripping pussy.

"Riversong is locked down tight," Chadrick reported, his cock throbbing as the Omega cried out. The Warlord's fingers had found a nipple and were abusing the tender bud. "None have come in or out, and there has been no sign of them in the streets between our territories. It seems they are not interested in clashing with us again."

Just as the Warguard was not interested in clashing with them, but he held his tongue on that observation. Morale was incredibly low among the Warguard, between their heavy losses and Morpheus' execution. The only ones who were happy were the young Alphas who had been promoted into the guard, but that had come with its own headaches as the more experienced guard sneered at their youthful enthusiasm.

There had already been several fights.

"They're hiding something... we need to find out what." Jeffos' eyes gleamed, and the Omega whimpered as his hand pushed between her legs, her hips moving forward to rub herself against his fingers.

Chadrick grit his teeth. Morpheus had regularly been rewarded with the services of an Omega. He would be as well, and he was looking forward to sating his lusts. He'd hoped to receive one after Morpheus' execution, but the Warlord had deemed his promotion to Captain enough of a reward. Anything more had to be earned.

"I don't believe my son is dead."

The oft-repeated refrain set Chadrick's teeth on edge. The Warlord was supposed to be canny. Smarter than all of them. Stronger than the other Alphas. While he might be the last, Chadrick was starting to doubt the male's intelligence.

He'd learned better than to argue.

"The healers have reported the prisoner is ready to be questioned," he said, deflecting rather than leading the Warlord down the well-trodden path of obsessing over Jordan's fate. He'd been holding that tiny tidbit of information back during his report to be used at a moment such as this.

The Warlord surged to his feet, dumping the naked Omega on the floor. She moaned, eyes glassy, hands tugging at his pants as she crawled to him. The movement sent the air wafting around her, and all the Alphas in the room growled, shuddering as the scent of her arousal permeated the air.

If she wasn't in heat, she would be soon. Not that it mattered to Jeffos. The male's willpower was unprecedented, or his obsession with his son had him so firmly in its grip, ignoring the demands of his Alpha nature didn't affect him as badly.

"Here. You may have this." The Warlord kicked the Omega aside with his foot, not even glancing down as she whimpered and curled into a ball. "I would suggest taking her back to your rooms, though, unless you want to fight for her." He laughed as he exited the room.

Chadrick didn't think twice, scooping the naked Omega up in his arms and enjoying the way she nuzzled into him. It didn't matter that it was due to her incipient heat. She was soft, smooth, and fit snugly against his chest. Dashing through the halls, he carried her to his rooms, eager to enjoy his reward.

ZADIA

The fever was gone, and her aches and pains had dwindled enough, she was able to concentrate on attempting to pick the lock on the chains around her wrists, securing her to the bed.

The position of vulnerability didn't sit well with her, and she knew it was only a matter of time before the questioning began. That they'd taken the time to heal her and allow her to recover first did nothing for her confidence.

The momentary sound of rapidly approaching footsteps was on her only warning before the door slammed open. A male stood in the entry, eyes wild and alight with glee.

Zadia froze.

The sheer amount of power emanating from him reminded her of Malachi, but there was something more. Malachi's presence was comforting, a protector's power.

This male was pure predator.

"Hello there." He smiled, stepping through the doorway and closing it behind him. "I'm so glad you're awake. Welcome to my home. I can't wait to get to know you."

Despite her conviction that no one could do nothing to make her betray her people, Zadia's mouth went dry with fear.

20

THE QUEEN

Tatiana

Despite the rapidly moving plans to rescue Zadia, there was only so long Tatiana could escape Malachi's notice.

"What's wrong?" Were the first words out of his mouth when he found her hunched against the toilet. The cramping pain that had begun not long after she'd taken the first suppressor pill made her retch before she could respond to him.

"Nothing." She didn't know why she bothered since it was incredibly, stupidly obvious something was very wrong, but that was her initial instinct.

"Try again." Malachi's voice was gentle. She heard water running, then a cool, wet cloth was pressed against her forehead. "The truth this time."

"I started taking suppressors." A shudder wracked her body. She wasn't sure this was any better than the heat, though she supposed it couldn't last forever. Otherwise, no one in the zones would be able to function.

There was a long pause, and she didn't dare look up at him. In this case, the need to lean against the toilet was a mercy. Taking them, she felt as if she'd failed him—them—but it was for the best. Already, her weakness had led to Zadia's capture, not to mention all the deaths.

Perhaps it was arrogance to think Malachi's presence could have made that much of a difference, but she truly believed it to be so. Which meant it was her fault Zadia had been taken, and who knew what was happening to her now that the Warlord had her in his clutches.

"Why?" The question was quiet, almost lethal, with barely suppressed emotion packed into that single word, but she couldn't tell what emotion. It didn't matter. Either way, she knew what sacrifices she was willing to make and what she wasn't willing to give up.

"This way, we won't have to worry my heat will interrupt things for you again... that it will happen at the worst possible time." Her voice faltered as a sob caught in the back of her throat. "No one else will pay because... because..."

"Shh." His strong hand rubbed the back of her neck, and she sighed. Between the cloth and the massage, she felt a little better. Physically, at least. "Nothing that happened was your fault."

They would never agree about that.

"Regardless, it won't happen again," she said, unable to keep the bitterness from her voice. "I will not be your liability."

Fingers ran through her hair, and he purred, the same purr that usually comforted her with its rumble. Tatiana's body revolted. The ache in her gut exploded even as her muscles tightened and shuddered. Dry heaving into the toilet again, tears stung her eyes as her body demanded she expel the contents of her stomach, but there was nothing left.

The rumble cut off abruptly with a curse. Malachi's hands gently cradled her. She could feel the tension in his body as he fought his instincts, which would tell him to purr and comfort her.

She couldn't take it right now. Something about the suppressors was reacting to his purr. There was no other explanation.

Holding himself around her, it must have been as painful for him not to make a sound as it had been for her to hear it. Every instinct would scream at him to soothe her, comfort her... and he couldn't. Not in the way he was supposed to.

"Go." She choked out the word between heaves, waving her hand at him. "Just go."

"Never."

GRIGORI

Humming tunelessly under his breath, Grigori skittered along the rooftops in the Warlord's territory. The new Captain of the Warguard was useless. His Warguard was making it so. None of them were patrolling where they were supposed to be, and he'd heard several of the guard resentfully grumbling about how he'd been gifted an Omega when the prisoner he'd brought in had awoken.

Which meant Zadia was still alive.

Which was important to know, though it didn't tell him where she was being held. Trying to get into the dungeons was a suicide mission—he didn't fool himself into thinking he'd be able to get out easily, no matter how lax the Warguard had become under their new command. He also knew the little deep reconnoitering he was doing would likely only be possible while the Warguard was still in turmoil.

Eventually, the new captain would get a handle on the situation, or he would be replaced by someone who would. Which came first relied on how much Jeffos was paying attention to his Warguards' dissatisfaction with the change in leadership.

"Oh where, oh where could she be." He wasn't sure he would share the information just yet, but he wanted to know.

The sudden sound of movement and voices coming from beneath him had him going silent and flattening himself on top of the roof. Thankfully, the roofs themselves were flat, and in the dwindling daylight, he would not easily be seen as long as he was still.

"Fucking Chadrick. You know he's balls deep in that Omega by now. As if he actually earned her."

Grigori rolled his eyes at the seething bitterness in the Alpha's voice. The way Alphas and Omegas were ruled by their instincts, they were truly no better than animals. They turned into unthinking beasts yet thought themselves superior.

He had little respect for his fellow Betas, either. So many of them accepted this ridiculousness instead of working to gain entrance to the zones, as he was. He wouldn't be trapped here in the territories much longer.

"It's only because the Warlord wants him out of the way while he questions the prisoner."

There was a pause.

"You might be right. Why do you think? Does he already not trust Chadrick?"

"I don't know, but he's not doing anything the usual way with this one. Did you hear he had her moved to his rooms?"

"What? Why?"

Their voices faded as they walked away, but Grigori had heard enough to know the first one didn't know the reasons behind Jeffos' decisions but had plenty of speculation. Speculating was something Grigori could do on his own, probably better than any of these muscle-brained idiots.

He assumed the prisoner they were discussing was Zadia—nothing else made sense—but why wasn't she in the dungeon? Why had she been moved?

Should he rush to tell Malachi and Cora and reap whatever reward they might have for such vital information, or should he wait to see what more information he could collect?

ZADIA

Feeling as if she must still be hallucinating, Zadia cautiously stepped around the Warlord into the grand room he'd led her to. Clutching the blanket he'd given her around her shoulders, she walked on trembling legs, aware of her vulnerability and that she was nowhere close to being healed.

"Much better accommodations, yes?"

The Alpha was playing with her, like a cat toying with a mouse because it wasn't hungry yet. She knew his mood could change with alacrity.

"Yes," she said, looking around. Having him at her back was making her tense, but she didn't know what else to do. Nothing happening was anything like what she'd expected. She'd thought he would torture her by now, perhaps show her some miserable prisoners and tell her that would be her fate if she didn't cooperate, or... something.

Not this.

"Again, I'm sorry you woke up in such poor conditions. My Warguard can be overzealous, and they did not understand my directions."

When Zadia turned to look at him, he was smiling, though it didn't reach his cold eyes. Not for one second did she believe a word out of his mouth but had to pretend she did. This was an unlooked-for opportunity. For whatever reason, the Warlord wanted to play head games, perhaps even try to win her to his side.

Cooperation would likely reap more rewards than fighting him and give her more time to heal, to put her in a position to escape. She didn't fool herself that she could learn anything Jordan hadn't already told Malachi, but at the very least, she could corroborate what the Warlord's son had told them. She didn't want to be in the Warlord's clutches any longer than she had to be.

The Alpha watched her, his muscular frame filling the doorway, eyes sharp and clear. If she didn't know what he was—who he was—she might have found him attractive. He could certainly pile on the charm when he put his mind to it, which made him all the more dangerous.

"Thank you," she finally said since he seemed to be waiting for a response. She still didn't know what she was doing here or what he wanted from her, other than information, but this was hardly the torture session she'd expected to endure.

"Are you hungry?"

Her stomach rumbled, and Zadia nodded. Was he going to feed her? She sensed a trap, but he was hardly going to poison her before questioning her. There were always people peddling things like truth serums on the black market, but she'd never seen any that worked.

After he ordered a meal through his comm unit, he went right back to watching her as she prowled the room. Unable to take his silent observation, she turned to face him. Legs trembling and the uncertainty of her situation gnawing at her, she was ready to defend herself if need be.

"What am I doing here, Jeffos?" She deliberately used his name rather than his title, hoping to provoke a more honest response.

To her surprise, he smiled, and the expression actually seemed genuine.

"You're here to become my Queen."

******

The Dawn of the Alpha trilogy continues in Waning Dawn.

ABOUT THE AUTHOR

Sinister Ange is a *USA Today* best-selling author and the alternate pen name for Golden Angel. She is happily married, old enough to know better but still too young to care, and a big fan of happily-ever-afters, strong heroes and heroines, and sizzling chemistry.

She believes the world is a better place when there's a little magic in it.

www.sinistreange.com

SINISTRE ANGE'S BOOKS

Dangerous Games

Calling Her Bluff
Forcing Her Hand
Claiming His Prize

Planets Apart

His Favorite Hucow: Hathor
Amaya's Old-Fashioned Daddy: Hebe
His Pretty Kitty: Seirios
Taking the Reins: Xanthos

Omegaverse

Rising Dawn
Waning Dawn
Darkest Dawn
His Omega Babygirl

. . .

Standalone Stories

Alien Pleasures
Annie and the Sybian
Consequences - Part 1
Consequences - Part 2
Naughty Coeds Boxset
Dark Tales Boxset
Dominated by the Bull

Black Light

Black Light: Roulette Rematch

Happily Never After with Raisa Greywood

Demon Lust
Blood Lust

Printed in Great Britain
by Amazon

23849444R00078